MW01042025

6 DINOSAUR DETECTIVE

Night of the Carnotaurus

To Mothra.—BBC

The author wishes to acknowledge the assistance of A. J. Johnson, who provided invaluable background information for the Hollywood aspect of this book.

6 DINOSAUR DETECTIVE

Night of the Carnotaurus

B. B. Calhoun

illustrated by Daniel Mark Duffy

Scientific American Books for Young Readers

W. H. FREEMAN AND COMPANY ◆ NEW YORK

Text copyright © 1995 by Christina Lowenstein
Illustrations copyright © 1995 by Daniel Mark Duffy

All rights reserved. No part of this book may be reproduced by any mechanical, photographic, or electronic process, or in the form of a phonographic or digital recording, nor may it be stored in a retrieval system, transmitted, or otherwise copied for public or private use, without the written permission of the publisher.

Book design by Debora Smith

Scientific American Books for Young Readers is an imprint of
W. H. Freeman and Company, 41 Madison Avenue
New York, New York 10010

This book was reviewed for scientific accuracy by Don Lessem,
founder of The Dinosaur Society.

Library of Congress Cataloging-in-Publication Data

Calhoun, B. B., 1961–

Night of the Carnotaurus/ B. B. Calhoun [i.e. Christina Lowenstein].

—(Dinosaur detective ; #6)

Summary: When Fenton Rumplemayer's father goes to Hollywood for a week as a technical consultant on a dinosaur film, Fenton accompanies him and discovers strange mistakes and accidents plaguing the movie studio.

ISBN 0-7167-6592-6 (hard). —ISBN 0-7167-6593-4 (pbk.)

[1. Dinosaurs—Fiction. 2. Paleontology—Fiction. 3. Motion pictures—Fiction. 4. Mystery and detective stories.] I. Title. II. Series: Calhoun, B. B. Dinosaur detective; #6.

PZ7.C12744Ni 1995

[Fic]—dc20

94-33631
CIP
AC

Printed in the United States of America.

10 9 8 7 6 5 4 3 2 1

1

"Just look at that," Fenton Rumplemayer said scornfully, his eyes on the television screen. "An apatosaurus fighting a triceratops. That's ridiculous."

"I think it's cool," said Willy Whitefox, who was sitting next to him on the overstuffed white leather couch. "Look how the triceratops uses its big horn like a sword."

"But the whole fight's impossible," said Fenton. "Those two dinosaurs lived eighty million years apart, as a matter of fact."

"Besides," added Maggie Carr from her spot on the white carpet in front of them, "why would two herbivores be fighting each other anyway? It's not like they want to eat each other." She turned to Fenton. "Hey, Fen, pass the popcorn."

Fenton picked up the bowl of popcorn, grabbed a handful, and passed it to her, his eyes still on the big-screen television in front of him. The apatosaurus was lying on its side now, and the triceratops was goring it in the stomach with its horns.

"Wow!" said Willy appreciatively.

Fenton had to admit the scene was exciting, even though it could never have taken place in real life. And sitting in Maggie's den, watching a movie on her big-screen TV, was a good way to spend a Saturday, especially now that it was so cold out.

Up until a few weeks earlier, Fenton had spent most of his free time out at Sleeping Bear Mountain, helping his father's dig team uncover dinosaur fossils. Both of Fenton's parents were paleontologists, scientists who study dinosaur bones, and until the past summer, the Rumplemayers had all lived in New York. But then Mrs. Rumplemayer had received a grant to study dinosaur bones in India, and Mr. Rumplemayer had been sent out to head the Sleeping Bear dig site in Morgan, Wyoming. Since moving to Morgan with his father, Fenton had helped the paleontologists solve several dinosaur mysteries out at Sleeping Bear. But now that winter was on its way, the team had closed up the dig site and begun working indoors, at the paleontology lab of the Flint campus of Wyoming State University, about fifteen miles away.

"Well, that's the end of the apatosaurus," Maggie commented.

On the screen the apatosaurus let out one last moan and lay on its side, perfectly still. The triceratops trotted off, and a shaggy-haired caveman dressed in an animal skin, a club over his shoulder, crawled cautiously out from behind a rock.

"Now *that's* crazy," said Fenton. "There weren't any humans until over sixty million years after the dinosaurs went extinct."

"I know," said Maggie. "But they always seem to put them in these old dinosaur movies."

"I wonder why," said Willy.

"I guess they figure people won't know any better or something," said Maggie. "You know, a lot of people don't really know that much about dinosaurs to begin with."

"And they certainly won't learn anything from watching

movies like this," said Fenton, as the caveman poked at the dead apatosaurus with his club. "What's this thing called again?"

"*Dawn of the Ages,*" said Willy. "It was the only dinosaur movie they had at Morgan Video."

Maggie's older sister, Lila, poked her head into the room.

"How much longer are you guys going to sit there in front of the TV?" she asked in an exasperated tone.

"Lila, we just started watching this movie," said Maggie. "We've got at least an hour and a half to go."

"Oh, great," sighed Lila. "Rob's coming over, and the football game is on." Rob was Lila's boyfriend. They were always together.

"So watch it on the little TV," said Maggie.

"In the kitchen?" asked Lila incredulously. "No way! Why can't you guys just watch your stupid movie some other time?"

"Because," said Maggie smugly, reaching for another handful of popcorn, "we got here first."

Lila closed the door with a slam, and Maggie nodded her head toward the television screen, where a screaming cavewoman was trapped in the jaws of a tyrannosaurus rex.

"What do you think?" said Maggie with a grin. "Does she look a little like Lila?"

They all snickered.

Two hours later, as the movie ended with a massacre of cavemen by the T-rex, Fenton turned to look out the window.

"Hey, look," he said. "It's snowing again."

"So?" said Maggie, her eyes still on the movie. "It snows all winter here, Fen. You'd better get used to it."

"Yeah," said Willy, laughing. "By the time it all thaws in the

spring, you'll probably forget what the ground looks like."

"When, exactly, does it thaw?" asked Fenton, thinking of the dig site. He was eager to get out there again, and the idea of a long winter without digging for dinosaurs didn't make him very happy.

"In the spring," said Maggie, hitting the rewind button on the remote control. "The snow should be gone by April or May."

"April or May?" Fenton repeated incredulously. In New York, the snow usually melted or turned to slush within hours after it hit the ground, and it hardly ever snowed after February. "You mean we might not get back out to the dig site until April or May?"

"Who knows?" said Maggie, shrugging. "Maybe we'll have an early thaw this year. After all, it was a pretty warm fall."

"Yeah," said Willy. "Usually it snows tons more than this."

Fenton shook his head in amazement. He'd already seen more snow in the past few weeks in Morgan than he usually saw in New York in an entire winter.

"Hey," said Maggie, grinning as the VCR clicked to a stop, "want to watch it again, just to drive Lila crazy?"

"I'd better not," said Fenton, glancing outside again. The sky was getting quite dark. "My dad's expecting me for dinner."

"I'd better get home too," said Willy. "We're having my mom's special sloppy joes tonight, and my dad's making french fries."

"Mmm," said Fenton. "Sounds good." He wondered what his own father was planning for dinner. Mr. Rumplemayer wasn't much of a cook, so if he and Fenton weren't pitching in together to follow one of Mrs. Rumplemayer's recipes, they usually ended up eating frozen or canned food.

"I think Dina's making meat loaf," said Maggie. Dina was the cook at the Carr Ranch. "Well, I guess I'll go find one of the ranch hands to drive me into town to return the video. We can drop you guys off on the way."

Ten minutes later Fenton was buckling his seat belt across his thick blue parka as the old Jeep they were sitting in took off down the bumpy driveway toward the gates of the ranch. Maggie sat in the front seat next to Zeke, one of the hands who helped take care of the ranch's horses, and Willy sat in the back, next to Fenton.

Maggie twisted in her seat to face the two boys. "Hey, what do you say we do this again next weekend, guys?"

"Okay," said Willy. "I'll get my dad to drive me into town again so I can pick up another video. Hey, maybe I can even get *Deadly Justice.*"

"That's that action-adventure movie with Van Steele, isn't it?" said Maggie. "The one that was playing at the Morgan Cinema last year?"

"That's right," said Willy enthusiastically. "It was fantastic. Van Steele is the greatest."

"Yeah, that was a pretty good movie," agreed Fenton, who had seen it back in New York with his friend Max Bellman.

"But we shouldn't rent it if both of you guys have already seen it," said Maggie.

"That's okay," said Willy quickly. "I want to see it again. You don't mind, do you, Fenton?"

Fenton shrugged. "It's okay with me, I guess."

They approached the turnoff for Willy's and Fenton's houses.

"It's right up here on the left, Zeke," Maggie instructed.

"Sure you kids don't want me to take you up the drive?" asked Zeke, pulling up to the turnoff.

"Nah, that's all right. We can walk," said Willy, opening the car door. "Thanks a lot for the ride."

"Yeah, thanks," said Fenton. "See you in school on Monday, Maggie."

"Okay, bye," said Maggie.

Fenton and Willy made their way up the snow-covered road. The snow was really coming down now; it looked like they would get at least a couple of feet on the ground before it was over. They arrived at Fenton's driveway, and Fenton waved to Willy and trudged up the hill toward the white house with the green shutters where he and his father lived. A light was on in the study window, and Fenton assumed that his father was up there working on something.

Fenton entered the house through the side door and left his wet boots and jacket in the entryway. His dog, Owen, came bounding into the kitchen to greet him.

"Hi there, boy," said Fenton, reaching down to scratch Owen behind the ears.

Fenton looked around the kitchen. It didn't seem as though his father had started dinner yet. There weren't any pots on the stove, and Fenton didn't smell anything warming in the oven. He grabbed an apple from the bowl on the kitchen table and decided to go upstairs.

As Fenton walked into the study with Owen close behind him, he saw that his father was on the telephone. Whomever he was talking to, Mr. Rumplemayer seemed very involved in his conversation. He didn't even look up when Fenton came in the room.

"Yes, I see," Mr. Rumplemayer was saying into the telephone. "Well, of course, that's a terrible misfortune. But I'm really not certain what it is you want me to do for you."

Fenton sat down in the empty chair, bit into his apple, and glanced at his watch. Five forty. In another twenty minutes it would be time to contact his friend Max back in New York by computer modem. Max was a computer genius. He had invented a computer game called Treasure Quest, and the two boys connected their computers every Saturday evening by modem so they could play it together.

"Well, what exactly would be involved?" said Mr. Rumplemayer. "I've never really done this sort of thing before, you know. How long would you want me to come out there for?"

Fenton turned to look at his father. Who was he talking to, anyway? It sounded as if he was planning a trip.

Mr. Rumplemayer picked up a pencil and began to scribble something on a pad of paper in front of him.

"That soon?" he said. "Well, of course, it's all a bit sudden, but I suppose I can manage it. Winter is generally the slow season in my line of work, and I do understand that you're in a bit of a bind. . . . Yes, certainly, Ms. Cagney. I'm glad to help out. . . . Well, it's been very nice talking to you, too." He hung up the phone and turned to face Fenton. "Oh, hello, son."

"Hi, Dad," said Fenton. "Who was that?"

"That," said his father, scratching his chin, "was Constance Cagney."

"Constance Cagney? Who's that?" asked Fenton. He finished off his apple and tossed the core into the wastebasket.

"She's a film director and producer," said his father. "Out in Hollywood. The daughter of Charles Cagney, the famous director from years ago."

Fenton shrugged. He had no idea who either of these people were.

"Anyway," his father went on, "she's making a movie about dinosaurs, and she's asked me to be the scientific advisor, to make sure that the dinosaurs are presented in an accurate way."

"Wow, that's great, Dad!" said Fenton. "You know, Willy and Maggie and I were just watching this movie today called *Dawn of the Ages*, and all the dinosaur stuff in it was totally wrong. I mean, they had a triceratops fighting with an apatosaurus, and a bunch of silly stuff like that. They even had cavemen in the same scenes with dinosaurs—"

"Hold on, hold on, Fenton," said his father, cutting him off. "Let me just think a moment. Now, apparently the original scientific advisor for this film had some sort of accident, so Ms. Cagney would like me to come out to Hollywood to replace him as soon as possible. But there are quite a few things to organize first. I'd probably be gone for about a week. Do you think Willy's parents might agree to let you stay at their house while I'm away?"

"No way!" said Fenton indignantly. How could his father think of going out to Hollywood without him?

Mr. Rumplemayer looked surprised. "But I thought you two were such good friends," he said. "You're always eating over there, and they've even had you overnight a few times. You don't think they'd agree?"

"Dad, that's not it," said Fenton in an exasperated voice. "I want to go to Hollywood with you!"

"Go with me?" said his father. "But what about school?"

"It's only a week," Fenton pointed out. "And I'm sure I can keep up with the work while I'm gone." Then he thought of something. "Besides, going out to Hollywood will be educational for me. I mean, you're going to be helping them out with all that dinosaur stuff, so I'm sure I'll learn something."

Fenton's father looked at him skeptically.

"Son," he said, "at this point, the last area of your education I think you need to be concerned with is your knowledge of dinosaurs."

Fenton shrugged sheepishly. He knew his father was right; Fenton already knew practically everything there was to know about dinosaurs.

"But . . . " his father said slowly, "perhaps it *would* be something of an educational experience for you to see another part of the country and get a look at how a film is made."

"Yippee! You mean I can go?" said Fenton, jumping up happily.

"Hold on just a minute," said his father. "I still want to think about this. And I'd like to talk it over with your mother. She said she'd try to call this weekend." He picked up the pad from his desk and looked down at the notes he had made. "Meanwhile, let me ask *you* something. Who is Kim Alexander?"

"Oh, she was in that movie *Wild Wheels*, about the race-car drivers," said Fenton.

"I see," said Fenton's father. "I guess I must have missed that one. Well, Constance Cagney says that Kim Alexander is in this dinosaur movie. Along with someone named Van Steele."

"Van Steele!" said Fenton. "Oh, wow, wait till Willy finds out. He loves Van Steele. Dad, this is great!"

Just then the fax machine next to the telephone rang and began to print something.

"Hey," said Fenton, "a fax. Maybe it's from Mom."

Mrs. Rumplemayer occasionally faxed them letters from India. Fenton loved getting mail this way because it arrived immediately, which meant that he could read one of his mother's letters moments after she had written it.

"Actually, it's probably from Ms. Cagney," said his father. "She said she was going to fax me some of the script for the movie so I could start looking at it right away."

Fenton walked over to the fax machine. The first page had finished printing, and he pulled it out and saw that it was the title page of the script. It said:

NIGHT OF THE CARNOTAURUS

✶ ✶ ✶

A GALAXY STUDIOS FILM

STARRING KIM ALEXANDER AND VAN STEELE

Produced and Directed by Constance Cagney

Night of the Carnotaurus, Fenton repeated to himself happily. This sounded great! Now all he had to do was convince his father to let him go.

2

"Fenton, you must be the luckiest kid on the whole planet," said Willy. "I can't believe you're actually going to get to meet Van Steele! In person!"

"Just think," said Maggie, "while I'm taking the vocabulary test on Monday with Mr. Wiley, you'll be hanging around with movie stars in California!"

It was the following Saturday, and Fenton, Willy, and Maggie were wrapped in thick wool blankets in the back of one of the green Wyoming State University pickup trucks that Fenton's father's dig team used. Curled up next to Fenton was Owen, and sitting in the front of the truck were Fenton's father and Charlie Smalls, one of the members of Mr. Rumplemayer's paleontological team. Charlie, who would be taking care of Owen while Fenton and his father were gone, had agreed to drive the Rumplemayers to the airport in Cheyenne for their flight to Los Angeles. Maggie and Willy had come along for the ride.

Fenton rubbed his gloved hands together and exhaled into them. Even though the truck's winter hardtop cover offered protection from the wind, the back of the truck was unheated, and

Fenton felt chilly. He tucked his feet under Owen and wrapped the blanket around himself more tightly.

"I'm still going to have to take that test when I come back, though, Maggie," he pointed out. "And I'll probably have to stay after school to do it."

"It's still worth it," said Maggie.

"Definitely," agreed Willy. "I'd stay after school for a whole year to meet Van Steele. He must be the toughest guy in the movies! I wish we could go with you."

"Yeah, me too," said Fenton. "But I'm lucky my dad let *me* go."

"Hey," said Willy. "Maybe we could hide in your suitcase or something." He laughed.

"Yeah," said Maggie. "Kind of like the Trojan horse."

"What's that?" asked Fenton.

"The Trojan horse," Maggie repeated. "I read all about it in this book about Troy I just finished."

"Troy?" said Willy. "Who's that?"

"Not who, *what,*" Maggie corrected. "Actually, *where.* Troy was the name of an ancient city that was at war with the Greeks."

"What happened?" asked Fenton.

"Well," said Maggie, "the Greeks needed to figure out a way to get inside the walls of the city, so they hid all their soldiers inside this giant statue of a horse on wheels, and then they sent it to Troy as a present. After the statue was wheeled past the gate and into the city, the soldiers leaped out in a surprise attack."

"That's pretty cool," said Willy. "It kind of reminds me of this *Morph Man* comic book where Morph Man had to get inside a lab where some bad guys were building a secret weapon. He found out that they were expecting a delivery of some weapons parts to the lab, so he morphed into a paper address label and stuck himself on one of the boxes. Then, once he was inside, he morphed back into himself and beat everybody up."

Fenton smiled. Willy was really into comic books. He had a huge collection of them, and he read them all the time.

Just then the truck pulled to a stop. Fenton peered out of one of the tiny windows of the hardtop and saw that they had arrived at the airport.

"We're here," he announced happily, feeling his heart begin to speed up a little with excitement.

A couple of hours later, Fenton and his father arrived at the Los Angeles airport, where they were greeted by a short, thickly built older man with a reddish face and a tangle of gray hair. The man was dressed in blue work pants and a dark blue windbreaker printed in white with the words GALAXY STUDIOS surrounded by a circle of stars.

"Hello," said the man in a raspy voice. "I'm Tom Williams. The studio sent me over to meet you folks."

"Oh, good," said Fenton's father. "I'm Bill Rumplemayer and this is my son, Fenton."

"Pleased to meet you," said Tom with a nod. "The car and the driver are just outside."

The first thing Fenton noticed as he and his father carried their two small suitcases out of the airport behind Tom was the weather. It was practically like a spring day. The sun was shining, and there was a faint breeze. Fenton was glad that Charlie had offered to take their winter parkas for them back at the Cheyenne airport. Looking around at the people milling about in their thin sweaters and light jackets, Fenton thought that the Morgan snow suddenly seemed very far away.

They followed Tom to a dark blue station wagon. The driver, a young, dark-haired man who introduced himself as Jeff, threw the suitcases into the back. Tom got into the front next to Jeff, and Fenton and his father climbed into the backseat.

They drove out of the airport and onto a huge highway filled with cars. Fenton peered out of the window, curious to see the city. But all he could make out beyond the broad highway were billboards, traffic signs, and ramps to other highways. Finally he saw a cluster of skyscrapers in the distance. The small clump of tall buildings almost reminded him of New York, except that it looked as though it was only a few blocks long.

"Is *that* Los Angeles?" Fenton asked in disbelief.

Tom chuckled. "That there is called downtown, but it's *all* Los Angeles," he said, sweeping an arm in an arc at the highway around them. "Just a bunch of crowded highways filled with cars." He shook his head. "She wasn't always this way, though."

"Yes, I hear there was a fairly good trolley system here once," said Fenton's father.

"There sure was," said Tom. "Back in the good old days, when the big studios like Galaxy, Summit, and Worldwide made good, wholesome pictures. Back then the directors had style and the stars had glamour." He shook his head again. "Things sure have changed, though. Here, this is our exit."

Jeff pulled off the highway at the exit marked Hollywood—Galaxy Studios. They drove down a wide, palm-lined boulevard and stopped in front of a huge metal gate with the Galaxy insignia on it. Next to the gate was a small booth with a guard dressed in a dark blue uniform. The guard waved to Jeff and Tom, and the gate opened.

Inside the gate was wide road lined with short, wide, white buildings.

"This here's called the Milky Way," said Tom. "All the streets in the studio are named like that; we've got the Milky Way, Saturn Street, Constellation Avenue. I guess somebody thought it'd be cute. All this stuff is new, though. None of it was around when I first started here."

"When did you first start working at Galaxy?" asked Fenton's father.

"June 19, 1938," Tom answered. "Been here ever since, 'cept for a tour overseas. Here at Galaxy, I done a little bit of everything. Why, some of the directors here, they couldn't get a movie made without me around to help them out. Hey, how'd you folks like a little tour before we head over to the offices? I could show you where some of the old Galaxy classics were made."

"Sure, that'd be fine," said Fenton's father. "That is, if you don't think Ms. Cagney will mind."

"She won't even notice," said Tom, as they pulled over. "She's got so many problems on this movie, she doesn't know whether she's coming or going."

They got out of the car and said good-bye to Jeff, who drove off, saying he'd leave their suitcases for them at their hotel.

GALAXY STU

"What kind of problems?" asked Fenton.

"Oh, just something with the dinosaurs," said Tom. "Or so I hear."

"With the dinosaurs?" Fenton repeated, interested.

"Yup," said Tom. "That's what they tell me. And things broken, a few damaged sets, some accidents. You know, that sort of thing."

"Oh yes," said Fenton's father. "Ms. Cagney did mention that the original science advisor, Dr. Beech, had been injured."

"Broke his leg," said Tom. "Well, once in a while you get a movie where everything goes wrong like that. What they used to call a jinx in the old days. Takes a real good director to handle it."

"But there's not really any such thing as jinxes," said Fenton.

"Maybe not," said Tom with a shrug. He led them toward a large wooden gate. "We can go in this way and take a look at the lots. See settings from your favorite old movies."

Tom opened the gate. Inside, Fenton was amazed by what he saw. There, right in front of them, was what appeared to be part of an old Western town, complete with dusty streets, sagging wooden porches, and a double-door saloon. All that was missing was the cowboys.

"Well, would you look at this!" exclaimed Fenton's father.

"This here's where they filmed *Guns of Dodge City,*" said Tom.

"Really!" said Fenton's father. "No kidding!"

"What's *Guns of . . .* whatever?" asked Fenton.

"*Guns of Dodge City,*" said his father. "It was a great old Western. I remember seeing it when I was a child."

"Yeah, don't make them like that anymore," said Tom.

"I suppose not," said Mr. Rumplemayer.

As they strolled down the street of the Western "town," it was hard for Fenton to believe that all of the buildings around him had been built just for the movies. It all seemed so real. Wait until he told Maggie and Willy about this.

Fenton went to peer through the window of what looked like a barbershop. As he did, he was surprised to see that there was nothing inside, not even a room. The "barbershop" was actually nothing more than a few pieces of wood and glass assembled and painted to look like the front of a building.

"False fronts," Tom informed him. "Only shoot outdoor scenes here. Indoor stuff is shot inside on the soundstages, those white buildings."

Fenton nodded. He supposed that made sense.

Tom led them around a corner, and suddenly the entire scene changed. They were no longer in a small Western town but were walking down what appeared to be a New York City street, complete with sidewalks, trees in plots of dirt, and buildings with front stoops.

"Hey!" said Fenton. "This looks just like home!"

"You folks from New York?" asked Tom.

"Yes, well, originally," said Fenton's father.

"Galaxy's little bit of New York," Tom explained with a sweep of his hand. "If a movie calls for New York City, the director can film it all right here."

"Wow," said Fenton, looking around. "This is amazing. It looks kind of like one of the streets in our old neighborhood."

"Very interesting," agreed Fenton's father. "But I suppose we should probably be getting over to Ms. Cagney now. I mean, she must be expecting us."

"I suppose," said Tom. He looked around. "Now, where's that passageway that takes us over to the executive offices?"

"Couldn't we just go back to the main road?" asked Mr. Rumplemayer.

"Oh, no, this way's much faster," Tom assured him. "Takes you right there." He turned his head from side to side again. "That short-cut, I think she's over here."

Fenton and his father followed Tom around the corner of the New York street and down an alley between two large white buildings. When they emerged from the alley, they came upon another deserted street, this one filled with sidewalk cafés and bakeries.

"This here's Galaxy's Paris," Tom explained. "You know, they filmed *Honeymoon in Paris* here. Great old movie, that was. Now, let's see, I think we go this way."

They left the Paris street and made their way through several more alleys, as well as a small-town America street, a modern London street, and a turn-of-the-century street complete with cobblestones and old-fashioned gas lanterns.

Finally Mr. Rumplemayer turned to Tom with an exasperated expression on his face.

"Are you certain you know where you're going?" he asked. "Because if not—"

"Why of course," said Tom with a smile. "We're practically there." He led them around another corner, and a large white building appeared in front of them. "Here we go," he said. "Galaxy Studios' executive offices."

3

Inside the building, Tom waved to another guard and took the Rumplemayers up in the elevator to the third floor. At the end of a long hall was a large wooden door with the Galaxy insignia. Underneath it was the name C. Cagney.

Tom rapped quickly on the door and pushed it open. Inside, a woman with short blond hair sat behind a large desk talking on the telephone. She looked up when she saw them come in.

"Okay, fine, Harry," she said into the telephone. "Look, do what you've got to do to fix it. I have to go now."

She hung up the telephone and walked over to where Fenton and his father were standing. "Mr. Rumplemayer?"

"Yes, hello," said Fenton's father, taking a step forward. "And this is my son, Fenton."

"Am I glad you're here," said Ms. Cagney, shaking Fenton's father's hand. "Pleasure to meet you, Fenton." She glanced down at her watch and frowned a little. "Hmm, it seems to be rather late. I had hoped you'd get here a little earlier so we could put you to work today. It seems we just keep losing more time on this movie. Frankly, at this rate, I'm beginning to wonder if it will *ever* get made."

"Yes, well, uh . . ." Mr. Rumplemayer began. He glanced at Tom, who had pulled out a toothpick and was picking his teeth.

"Well, the important thing is you're here now," said Ms. Cagney. She gestured to a large brown couch. "Please, have a seat. Tom, please bring our visitors something to drink."

Fenton and his father sat down on the couch, and Tom turned and shuffled from the room.

"I'm so glad you're here, Mr. Rumplemayer," Ms. Cagney said again. She sat down behind her desk. "Ever since we lost Dr. Beech, we've had nothing but trouble with this film."

"Yes," said Mr. Rumplemayer. "Tom mentioned that a few things had gone wrong."

"That's putting it mildly." She sighed. "We seem to be having particular trouble with the dinosaurs. Mistakes in the animation, lost or damaged models, you name it. Quite frankly, I'll be happy to see that aspect of it put back in the hands of a science professional."

"Well, I'll certainly do the best I can, Ms. Cagney," said Mr. Rumplemayer.

"Yeah, now that me and my dad are here, you don't have to worry about the dinosaurs at all," added Fenton.

Ms. Cagney smiled. "Well, I'm very happy to hear that."

Tom returned with two glasses of cold soda and handed them to Fenton and his father.

"You see," Ms. Cagney went on, "on this particular film, the scientific advisor is crucial. A scientific foundation has made a major investment in the film, but they've done so provided that the scientific details in the movie are absolutely correct."

"I understand," said Mr. Rumplemayer, nodding.

"It's a difficult task," Ms. Cagney went on. "As you know, the film is about time travelers who go back to the Mesozoic. It features many different types of dinosaurs, and it is essential that every detail be just right. This cannot be just another 'monster' movie with no regard for scientific accuracy."

"You mean like *Dawn of the Ages*?" said Fenton.

Ms. Cagney made a face. "Exactly, Fenton," she agreed. "Exactly what we're *not* going to do. That is, if we ever get this picture made." She looked over at Tom, who was standing by the door. "Well, Tom, why don't you show the Rumplemayers the technical building and the soundstage where we'll be shooting tomorrow. And then I suppose they'd like to get settled in at the Galaxy Hotel." She smiled. "You're in good hands with Tom, here. He's been with the studio for ages—bounced me on his knee when my father directed films here. Isn't that right, Tom?"

Tom nodded and grunted.

Yeah, well, for someone who's been here that long, he certainly doesn't seem to know his way around very well, thought Fenton. I hope he doesn't get lost trying to get us to the hotel.

But luckily, this time Tom had no trouble finding his way. After showing Fenton and his father the technical building, a large white building on Jupiter Lane, he took them next door to Soundstage 3.

"Where they'll be shooting tomorrow," he informed them.

Fenton looked around the enormous room. The ceiling was covered in a web of cables, metal beams, and lighting equipment, and there were several large cameras, two of them mounted on cranes. In the center of the room was what appeared to be a capsule of some sort. It was white, and approximately seven feet tall, with windows running around it and a dome on top.

"What's that?" asked Fenton.

"Oh, she's the time machine they travel in," explained Tom. "You know, to get back to the dinosaurs. They're filming some scenes with her tomorrow."

"Hmm. Yes, I see," said Fenton's father.

"Van Steele's going to be here tomorrow?" asked Fenton.

"That's right," said Tom, pointing. "There's his chair."

Fenton turned and saw four tall, dark blue canvas chairs behind him. One was printed with Constance Cagney's name, another with Van Steele's, and the third with Kim Alexander's. Printed on the fourth chair was the name Justin Cho.

"Justin Cho, who's that?" Fenton asked, pointing at the chair.

"The kid," said Tom.

"The kid?" Fenton repeated.

"Yeah, the kid actor in the film," said Tom. "He plays Nick. Must be about your age, actually. You'll meet him tomorrow."

Fenton knew from looking over the portions of the script that Ms. Cagney had faxed to his father that there was a character named Nick in the film, but he hadn't realized that the character was a child. It would be fun to have someone else his age on the movie set to hang out with, Fenton decided.

Tom took them back to the car to pick up their bags and showed them the way to the Galaxy Hotel, a sprawling glass-and-concrete building right next to the studio grounds. Fenton and his father settled into their room, which had two large beds and was decorated in the Galaxy colors—dark blue and white. After unpacking a couple of things, Mr. Rumplemayer said he wanted to take a shower before they went down to the hotel's restaurant for dinner. Fenton helped himself to a soda from the room's mini-refrigerator and lay across one of the beds with a book he had brought from home, *The Pocket Book of One Thousand Interesting Dinosaur Facts,* open in front of him.

But try as he might, Fenton couldn't seem to concentrate. The book was one of his favorites, but tonight it just wasn't holding his attention. Finally he put it down and walked over to the window.

Fenton gazed out at the gates of the studios and the little guardhouse, and beyond it to the broad illuminated expanse of Milky Way. He couldn't believe his good luck. Here he was in Hollywood, missing a week of cold weather and school back in Morgan. And tomorrow he'd get a behind-the-scenes look at a film about dinosaurs and get to meet Van Steele and the others, too! Fenton couldn't wait.

4

The following morning Fenton accompanied his father to the computer-animation department of the Galaxy technical building. The room, which had two long desks running along either side of it, was filled with computers, several of them with people working at them. Fenton thought of his friend Max back in New York. A roomful of computers would probably be Max's idea of a dream come true.

A short, dark-haired woman walked over to them.

"Hello," she said, putting out her hand. "You must be Bill Rumplemayer. I'm Rosa. Rosa Alvarez. I supervise the computer-generated dinosaur images for the film."

"Pleased to meet you, Rosa," said Mr. Rumplemayer. "This is my son, Fenton."

"Hello there, Fenton," said Rosa, smiling. "Perhaps I should start by giving you both a little background on what we do here. These people are at work creating computer drawings of the various dinosaurs that appear in the film. The images are based first on skeletal reconstructions, similar to the ones I imagine you paleontologists put together out in the field. Then we flesh them in to create realistic pictures of the dinosaurs."

Fenton nodded. This was the way he had often sketched dinosaurs back at the New York Museum of Natural History, by first copying the skeleton into his sketchbook and then filling in the flesh and outer skin over the bones. He hadn't realized that you could do it on a computer, though. That sounded like fun. He'd have to ask Max about it the next time they talked.

"Finally," Rosa went on, "we ask the computer to generate a large number of these images for each animal, each in a slightly different position. When we put them in sequence they create what we call 'motion patterns' and the animal seems to move."

"I see," said Fenton's father. He chuckled. "In my line of work, if you want to see a dinosaur move, you have to have a pretty vivid imagination."

Rosa laughed. "Well, one of the ways that we're able to analyze the animals' movements here in the lab is by using D.I.D.s."

"D.I.D.s?" Fenton repeated. "What are those?"

"D.I.D. stands for digital input device," Rosa explained. "Or *dinosaur* input device, if you like. I've got one right here, for the saltasaurus."

She walked over to a set of shelves mounted over one of the desks and took down what looked to Fenton like a four-legged robot. She put it down on the desk, and Fenton realized that what he was looking at was a crude-looking metal mechanical model of a saltasaurus, a large sauropod dinosaur from the Late Cretaceous whose fossils had been found in Argentina.

"The various body parts are designed to be moved by hand," Rosa explained as she manipulated one of the dinosaur's metal legs, "and the entire D.I.D. is linked electronically to a computer. That way the computer is able to record the movements and translate them into pictures."

"And that's how they put all the dinosaurs in the movie?" asked Fenton. "With D.I.D.s and computers?"

"Well, not all of them," said Rosa. "The final effects will be created by a combination of computer animation and some stop-motion 'claymation' models. They're also building a large-scale robotic model of one of the dinosaurs, the carnotaurus."

"Well, it sounds as if you've got it all figured out," said Mr. Rumplemayer. "Frankly, I'm not sure what it is you need me for."

"Well, Ms. Cagney's very concerned about the details on this," said Rosa as she put the sauropod D.I.D. back on the shelf. "Especially since we've had a few problems."

"What exactly happened?" asked Mr. Rumplemayer. "All I know is that things have been going wrong."

"There were some mistakes in the way some of the dinosaurs were represented," explained Rosa. "But I believe Dr. Beech was able to fix those before he left. And then for a while we were having some trouble with our computer, but that seems to have cleared up as well. But Ms. Cagney feels it's still important for us to have a scientist on board to verify the work we're doing here."

"All right, then," said Mr. Rumplemayer, "just tell me where you want me to begin."

"Sure," said Rosa. "As I said, Dr. Beech has already checked most of the dinosaurs on the computer, but if you'll come with me, I can let you take a look at the most recent images, the ones that were done after he left."

Mr. Rumplemayer joined Rosa at one of the computers, and Fenton explored the large room. As he walked around, a couple of the computer animators glanced up a him and smiled, but most of them seemed to be concentrating on their work. Displayed on several of the computer monitors that lined the desks were drawings of dinosaurs. Fenton stopped in front of an unattended computer and recognized the head of a gallimimus, a fast-moving, long-legged "ostrich dinosaur" from Mongolia. Another computer, where a young man with a beard was working, showed a carnotaurus, the double-horned T-rex–like dinosaur of the movie's title. Then, at the end of the row of computers, Fenton saw another dinosaur he recognized—or *thought* he recognized.

The dinosaur looked an awful lot like a huayangosaurus, a stegosaur from China. Fenton knew that huayangosaurus, which lived during the Middle Jurassic period of the age of dinosaurs, was relatively small and had a double row of spiky plates running down its back. But there was something else about huayangosaurus, something that set it apart from other, later, stegosaurs. And that something wasn't in this drawing.

Fenton peered more closely at the computer screen. He knew that an unusual feature of huayangosaurus was that its front legs were the same size as its hind legs. But this image seemed to show a dinosaur with legs that were shorter in the front than in the back, more like those of later stegosaurs. There was no doubt about it; there was definitely a problem.

"Dad?" said Fenton, shifting his eyes from the screen. He walked over to where his father and Rosa were studying a drawing of a telmatosaurus, a Romanian duckbill dinosaur. "Dad," he said again, "I think there's a problem with one of these dinosaur drawings over here."

"A problem?' said Rosa, looking alarmed. "What do you mean? You didn't touch any of the computers, did you?"

"No, of course not," said Fenton. "But there's definitely something wrong with your huayangosaurus."

"What's the trouble, son?" asked Mr. Rumplemayer.

"Come and see for yourself," said Fenton.

They walked over to the computer, and Fenton pointed at the dinosaur on the screen. "See? The front legs are too short, aren't they?"

"They certainly are," agreed Mr. Rumplemayer. "The front legs on this particular dinosaur should be the same length as the back ones," he explained to Rosa.

"But that's impossible!" Rosa exclaimed.

"Actually, I would say it's quite an understandable mistake," said Fenton's father. "You see, huayangosaurus is a stegosaur, and all the later stegosaurs do have legs like this. These legs just look like they belong on a kentrosaurus or a stegosaurus rather than on a huayangosaurus." He turned to Fenton. "Good eye, son."

"I simply can't believe it," said Rosa, shaking her head.

"Well, no harm done," said Mr. Rumplemayer. "Anyway, I'm sure I would have caught the error when we reviewed the images for this dinosaur."

"But that's just the thing!" Rosa exclaimed. "The images for that dinosaur *have* been reviewed—by Dr. Beech! He went over all the pictures for the huayangosaurus before he got hurt."

"Well, I guess he missed this somehow," said Fenton.

"Yes, I supposed he must have overlooked it," said his father. "It happens to the best of us, you know. Even a professional can make an error like this."

"Well then, I'm just glad you caught it," said Rosa. "I tell you, I've never heard of a film where there were so many problems. We're already weeks behind schedule. Of course, for me, that just means I have a steady job for longer."

"Oh, you mean your job's over when the film's completed?" asked Mr. Rumplemayer.

Rosa nodded. "Unless they want to hire me for another movie. You see, I work freelance, so I get hired for one picture at a time," she explained. "Anyway, I'll have Alex, the animator who's been working on this, fix it as soon as he gets in. I suppose I should thank you, Fenton."

"No problem," said Fenton. He was glad he'd been able to catch the mistake. It was probably just the kind of thing Ms. Cagney had been talking about when she'd said it was essential that every detail of the dinosaurs be scientifically correct.

Later that afternoon, Fenton stood alone in a corner of Soundstage 3. Beside him was an enormous floodlight on a stand, and at his feet lay a coil of cable. All around him people were rushing about, setting up various pieces of equipment. Mr. Rumplemayer had gone back after lunch to finish reviewing the computer graphics with Rosa Alvarez, and Fenton had decided to visit the soundstage to see if he would finally get a chance to meet the film's stars.

But so far there was no sign of Van Steele or Kim Alexander anywhere. Constance Cagney was there, talking intently with a man in overalls who was carrying a wooden ladder under one arm, and old Tom Williams was standing nearby, but neither of them seemed to have noticed Fenton. Fenton sighed. This wasn't exactly what he had in mind. In fact, it was pretty boring. He was starting to wish he had gone back with his father instead.

Fenton sat down on the coil of cable and pulled out *The Pocket Book of One Thousand Interesting Dinosaur Facts.* Now he was really glad that he had shoved it into his jean-jacket pocket before leaving the hotel that morning. Anything was better than just standing in the corner watching the crew set up equipment.

Fenton opened his book, and before he knew it, he was lost in his reading and had almost forgotten where he was. Then, just as he was getting to the end of a passage about spinosaurus, a spiny-backed Egyptian dinosaur that was one of the largest meat-eaters of all time, Fenton heard a voice above him.

"You really shouldn't sit there, you know."

Fenton raised his eyes from his book and saw a boy who looked around his age standing in front of him. The boy had short, shiny black hair, and he was dressed in a pair of colorful baggy shorts and a red T-shirt.

"You really shouldn't sit there," the boy said again. "Somebody might need to use that cable for something."

"Oh," said Fenton. He stood up. "I didn't realize. I mean, it didn't seem like anyone was using it. . . ."

"Well, you better not let Constance catch you in here," said the boy. "Outsiders aren't supposed to be allowed on the set when we're working."

"I'm not really an outsider," said Fenton. "I mean, my father's working on the dinosaurs for the movie, so Const— I mean, Ms.

Cagney said it was okay."

"Your dad's replacing that Dr. Beech guy who got hurt?" asked the boy.

"Right," said Fenton. He closed his book. "I'm Fenton. Fenton Rumplemayer."

"Hi," said the boy. "I'm Justin Cho."

"Oh, wow," said Fenton. "You're in the movie!"

"No kidding," said the boy. "So, are you staying at the Galaxy Hotel?"

"Yeah," said Fenton. "With my father."

"My mom and I are staying there too," said Justin. "What suite are you in?"

"Suite?" said Fenton.

"You know, what's the name on the plaque outside the door to your rooms?" asked Justin. "All the suites are named after planets. We're in the Mars suite."

"I don't think we're in a suite," said Fenton. "I mean, I think we're just in a regular room."

"Oh," said Justin. "Well, I guess the suites are only for the actors."

"Hey," said Fenton in a low voice. "Do you know Van Steele?"

"Of course I do," said Justin. "We're working together."

"Is he going to be here soon?" asked Fenton.

"Yeah, he's right there behind you," said Justin, pointing over Fenton's shoulder.

Fenton whipped around, but the only person behind him was a guy in jeans taping some electrical wire to the floor.

"Ha, ha!" said Justin, clutching his stomach. "You fell for it!"

"Yeah," said Fenton. "I guess I did."

"Hey, come on," said Justin. "No hard feelings. Here, have a stick of gum." He reached into his pocket and held out a pack to Fenton. But when Fenton reached for a piece, a small metal clip popped out of the pack and snapped against his finger.

"Ha, ha!" said Justin again. "Hey, what's the matter, can't you take a joke?" He reached into his pocket and tossed a square of bubble gum to Fenton. "Here, have a real one."

Fenton unwrapped the gum and popped it in his mouth. This kid had some sense of humor.

"So," said Fenton. "Have you been in any other movies?"

"Sure," said Justin with a yawn. "And a bunch of TV commercials, too. I started acting when I was three."

"I guess you do look kind of familiar," said Fenton. "Wow, being in the movies and stuff must be pretty cool."

"I guess," said Justin, looking bored. He reached for the book in Fenton's hands. "Hey, what's this?"

Fenton handed him the book.

"Oh," said Justin, reading the title. "Dinosaurs." He handed it back to Fenton.

"It's a really good book," Fenton told him.

"I guess, if you like dinosaurs," said Justin.

"You mean you're in this movie and you don't even like dinosaurs?" said Fenton incredulously, putting the book back in his jacket pocket.

"What's to like?" said Justin with a shrug. "Just a bunch of big old lizards." He paused. "Besides, they film all the dinosaur stuff separately. Hey, there's Van for real. And Kim, too."

Fenton turned around. Sure enough, on the other side of the room were the movie's two stars. Fenton would have recognized them anywhere. Kim Alexander, her wavy brown hair pulled into a ponytail and a pair of sunglasses perched on her head, was sitting in her canvas chair, studying what looked like a script and making marks on it with a red pen. Van Steele was standing next to her, running one hand through his closely cropped blond hair, a worried expression on his face.

Fenton had an idea. Maybe he should ask for Van's autograph to give to Willy. Willy would flip.

"Hey, Justin," he said. "Do you think Van Steele would give me his autograph? I have a friend back home who's a really big fan of his."

"Sure, he'd probably do it," said Justin. "Come on, let's go ask him."

They walked over to the two actors.

"Hi Kim. Hi Van," said Justin. "This is Fenton. His father's working on the movie."

Kim Alexander looked briefly up from her script. "Oh, hello," she said.

"Hi, there," said Van.

"Hi," said Fenton. "Um, Mr. Steele, I was wondering, do you think maybe I could have your autograph for a friend of mine?"

"Sure," said Van. "You got a piece of paper?"

Fenton dug into his jean jacket pockets. But all he had with him was his dinosaur book. Finally he tore out one of the blank pages near the end.

"Here," said Kim Alexander, handing over her pen. "Why

don't you use this."

But Van looked at the pen in horror. "I can't use that to sign my name!" he said.

"Why not?" asked Kim. "It's a perfectly good pen."

"But it's red!" said Van, pushing it back into her hands. "Don't you know that it's very bad luck to write your name in red ink?"

"Oh, come on," said Kim. "Don't be so superstitious. Give the kid an autograph."

"Not with a red pen I won't," said Van stubbornly.

"Here," said Kim. She took the piece of paper from Van, scribbled something on it, and handed it back to Fenton. "There you go."

Fenton looked down at the paper. There, scrawled in red ink, were the words:

To Franklin—
Best wishes, Kim Alexander

"Oh, uh, thanks," Fenton managed to say.

"Don't mention it," said Kim, her eyes back on her script.

"Signing with a red pen—you've got to be crazy to take a risk like that," Van muttered, shaking his head. "There's enough bad luck in to be found in this place without coming out and *asking* for it."

"Boy, that was weird," said Fenton as he and Justin walked away.

"Oh, don't listen to him," said Justin. "He's just a big chicken. He's scared of everything."

"But he seems so tough in the movies," said Fenton.

"It's all an act," said Justin. "He's incredibly superstitious." He grinned mischievously. "There's this black cat that wanders around the studio grounds sometimes, and the other day I brought it in here to the soundstage right before Van was supposed to shoot a scene. He took one look at it and went nuts! He was practically threatening to quit the movie. It was so funny!" He laughed.

"He almost quit the movie?" Fenton asked in amazement. "Didn't Ms. Cagney get mad at you?"

"Yeah, kind of," Justin answered. "But it was worth it just to see the look on Van's face. He's such a big baby. Did you know he walks around with this lucky rabbit's foot all the time, and he puts it in the pocket of whatever costume he's wearing? And if the costume doesn't have a pocket, he makes the wardrobe people sew one in!"

"Wow," said Fenton. Wait until Willy heard this. He wouldn't believe it.

"Yeah," said Justin. He laughed. "Just because a lot of stuff's been going wrong with the movie, Van's totally convinced the whole film's jinxed."

Fenton laughed too. Sure, everyone seemed to be talking about how many problems this movie had had, but Fenton knew for sure that there was no such thing as jinxes. After all, there was a logical explanation for everything if you knew where to look, and jinxes just weren't logical.

But then he began to think. If there was a logical explanation for everything, what was the logical explanation for all the problems on the set of *Night of the Carnotaurus*?

5

Later that evening Fenton lay in his bed in the hotel, leafing through *The Pocket Book of One Thousand Interesting Dinosaur Facts* while his father brushed his teeth in the bathroom. Fenton had spent the rest of that afternoon watching Ms. Cagney and the film crew shoot a scene where the actors were in the time capsule.

At first it had been pretty interesting, watching as Ms. Cagney gave Kim, Van, and Justin their instructions and then told the cameras to start rolling. The back of the capsule had been cut away so the cameras could film the actors inside, and it looked like fun crouching in there. Fenton had even started to feel a little jealous of Justin. After all, it must be a lot more exciting spending your days in front of a movie camera than sitting in school.

But by the time Ms. Cagney had had the actors do the same scene for about the twentieth time, even Fenton was starting to get bored. And then, when they finally stopped shooting a couple of hours later, and Justin told Fenton that he had to go report to his tutor for a math lesson, Fenton started feeling downright sorry for Justin. As Justin explained, child actors did go to school while they were making movies; Justin and his tutor managed to squeeze in their lessons between his scenes, using a trailer parked on one of the lots as a classroom. Fenton didn't think he'd like having a tutor and being the only kid in the class; it didn't sound like much fun. He supposed it wasn't too surprising that Justin was so into practical jokes. It must be one of the only ways he ever got to have a good time.

Fenton adjusted the pillow behind him and turned to the section in the book on carnotauruses. His father had told him that members of the crew were constructing the life-sized mechanical model of the carnotaurus that would be used in the film. Apparently Ms. Cagney planned to use a combination of computer animation and the robotic model for the film's climactic fight scene between the actors and the carnotaurus. Fenton laughed a little to himself, thinking about how movies always seemed to end up putting humans and dinosaurs together in the same scenes. But at least in this dinosaur movie it made more sense, he reminded himself, since the characters were supposed to have traveled back to the Mesozoic in a time capsule.

The drawing in the book showed a dinosaur that looked a bit like a tyrannosaurus but had two short horns protruding above its eyes. Carnotaurus was a sharp-toothed meat-eater that lived in the Middle to Late Cretaceous, 113 to 91 million years ago, and its remains had been found in Argentina. The interesting fact highlighted by the book was that carnotaurus's skin was covered with small bony bumps, something that scientists had learned from fossilized skin impressions discovered with carnotaurus bones.

Fenton's father came out of the bathroom in his pajamas.

"Whew, what a day," he sighed, climbing into his own bed. "I must have looked at dozens of dinosaur images. This moviemaking is a tough business."

"Did you find any more mistakes besides the huayangosaurus?" asked Fenton.

"Nope," said his father, settling down under the covers. "Everything looked a-okay."

"I guess that Dr. Beech guy only missed that one thing, then," said Fenton.

"Actually, Rosa and I decided it probably wasn't worth my going over any of the other pictures that Dr. Beech had already reviewed," said Mr. Rumplemayer.

"Why not?" said Fenton. "I mean, what if he made other mistakes?"

"I don't think that's too likely," said his father. "Dr. Beech is a well-known paleontologist at Rupert College in Montana. Rosa figures it was probably the animator who made the error. Rosa told me he's new there, and she's spoken to him and told him to be more careful." He yawned. "Okay, son, what do you say we turn off the light now? I'm bushed, and we should both get to sleep."

"Okay," said Fenton, putting his book on the night table.

Mr. Rumplemayer switched off the lamp. "Anyway," he said, "it doesn't seem worth the time it would take for me to go over all those computer images. Especially since they've already been reviewed by an expert."

"I guess," said Fenton into the darkness. But somehow he just couldn't seem to shake this nagging feeling that his father was wrong, that somebody should be looking very closely at the rest of the dinosaurs in the computer.

The following morning Fenton went with his father to the

model-making studio, which was directly across the hall from the computer-animation room. The studio was filled with paint-spattered worktables, and there were several people busy sculpting and painting dinosaur models. On one table Fenton spotted a hypsilophodon, a small, swift, lightly built plant-eater from the Early Cretaceous, as well as a small model of a carnotaurus.

"Hello," said a tall, thin man in a paint-smeared T-shirt and jeans. "You must be the Rumplemayers. I heard you were headed out my way today. I'm Harry. Harry Brown, head model maker for the project."

"Hello, Harry," said Fenton's father, shaking his hand. "I'm Bill, and this is my son, Fenton."

"Nice to meet you," said Harry. "Well, I suppose you'd like to take a look at the dinosaurs."

"Definitely," said Fenton enthusiastically.

They walked over to the table with the hypsilophodon. A woman in a gray smock was leaning over the one-foot-tall model, carefully sculpting scaly ridges into its skin with a small metal tool.

"Wow, this is really great," said Fenton, noting the details in the dinosaur model. In addition to textured skin, the model showed the hypsilophodon's beaklike mouth and tiny eye.

The woman who was working on it glanced up at Fenton and smiled.

"Yes, Galaxy's model-making studios are really state-of-the-art," said Harry. "They've, I mean, *we've* got all the latest equipment here for this sort of thing." He lowered his voice in a mock whisper. "I used to work for the competition, you know."

"The competition?" said Fenton.

"He means Worldwide," said the woman working on the model. "It's another film studio. Galaxy and Worldwide have always been rivals."

"This is my first film with Galaxy," Harry explained.

"Tell me, Harry. Just how, exactly, are you going to be using these models in the film?" asked Mr. Rumplemayer.

"Well," said Harry, "for certain scenes, particularly those that don't have human actors in them, Ms. Cagney wants to use these dinosaur models and film them with what's called stop-motion photography."

"What's that?" asked Fenton.

"We use a special type of camera that takes a sequence of pictures of the model," Harry explained. "In between shots we move the model to a slightly new position. Then, when you put all the pictures together in sequence the model appears to move."

"I get it," said Fenton.

"Is that what they call claymation?" asked Mr. Rumplemayer.

"It is sometimes called that," answered Harry. "Although the models are not made purely of clay. We're utilizing a variety of materials—latex, foam rubber, and fiberglass, as well as clay."

"I see," said Mr. Rumplemayer.

"When the models are finished," said Harry, leading them over to another area of the studio, "they're set out here on these shelves, and grouped according to which scenes they'll be used in."

Fenton looked at the dinosaurs lined up along the shelves on the wall. He recognized a bunch of gallimimuses, the Mongolian

"ostrich dinosaur" he had spotted on one of the computer screens the day before. And next to them were some bagaceratopses, small ceratopsian dinosaurs with short nose horns.

"What about the big carnotaurus model?" asked Fenton. "Can we see that now?"

"Actually, that's a different department," Harry explained. "The life-sized carnotaurus is an animatronic model—a mechanically operated one—so there are engineers and mechanical specialists working on it, in addition to artists. If you want to take a look, though, it's downstairs."

"Downstairs?" said Fenton.

"Sure," said Harry. "Just go down to the first floor and look for signs to the south wing."

"Can I go, Dad?" asked Fenton.

"Certainly, son," answered Mr. Rumplemayer. "I'm just going to look over a few more of these dinosaurs with Harry here."

Fenton took the elevator down to the first floor. The south wing turned out to be one enormous room, with an entire wall that opened up like a garage door onto Nova Street, which ran behind the building.

Standing in the middle of the room, partially encased in scaffolding, was the mechanical carnotaurus model. Fenton stared up at the huge unfinished dinosaur in awe. Fenton had seen plenty of upright, fully-assembled dinosaur skeletons back at the museum in New York, some of them a lot bigger than the twenty-five-foot-long carnotaurus. But gazing up at this lifelike reconstruction, with its bumpy brown skin, sharp toenail claws, and beady eyes, was really incredible. He almost felt as though he was looking at a live, but motionless, dinosaur.

Or *part* of a dinosaur, at least. The carnotaurus was incomplete; its arms hadn't been attached yet, and its tail was still skinless. A hatch door was open in the dinosaur's chest area, and someone in a pair of gray coveralls stood on a ladder, working inside it. Within the skinless metal "skeleton" of the tail, Fenton could see some machinery that he figured must make the dinosaur move. A couple of workers on metal scaffolding were perched by the creature's huge mouth, applying paint to the rows of sharp teeth.

"She's really something, huh?" said a raspy voice in Fenton's ear.

Fenton turned. Tom Williams was standing behind him, a can of paint in his hand.

"That's for sure." agreed Fenton.

Tom put down the paint can and shook his head. "Amazing to think that nowadays a big machine like this can actually be the star of a movie. Times sure have changed."

"Yeah, I guess," said Fenton.

Tom called up to the workers on the scaffolding who were painting the dinosaur's teeth. "Got your paint here, fellas!"

"Oh," said one of the workers, glancing down. "Thanks!"

"I'll bring it up to you," Tom said. He bent to pick up the paint can and carried it over to a large wooden A-frame ladder near the scaffolding.

As Tom climbed the ladder, Fenton gazed up at the workers painting the carnotaurus's teeth. Now *that* looked like a fun job, thought Fenton. Maybe even almost as fun as being a paleontologist.

Later that day, as Fenton and his father made their way down Jupiter Lane toward the Galaxy Studios commissary for lunch, they saw Justin coming the other way.

"Hi," said Fenton. "Dad, this is Justin. He's in the movie."

"Pleased to meet you, Justin," said Mr. Rumplemayer.

"Hi," said Justin. "You're working on the dinosaurs, right?"

"That's right," said Mr. Rumplemayer.

"Hey, Justin," said Fenton. "You want to come eat lunch with us at the commissary?"

"I can't," said Justin glumly. "I have to meet Mr. Twomble in my trailer for an English class."

"Oh," said Fenton.

"Speaking of school, I haven't noticed you cracking any books since we got here, son," said Fenton's father.

"Oh, Dad," groaned Fenton. How could his father expect him to concentrate on homework when there was so much other interesting stuff to see at Galaxy?

"Remember," said his father, "part of our agreement was that you were going to keep up with your assignments."

"I will, I will," said Fenton.

"I better go," said Justin. "But hey, if you're not doing anything after lunch, you really should come on over to the lot behind the soundstage building we were in yesterday. Constance is shooting one of Van's dinosaur fight scenes." He raised his eyebrows, and his eyes twinkled. "It should be a *lot* of fun."

"Oh, okay," said Fenton, waving as Justin walked off. "See you then."

A dinosaur fight scene sounded like fun, thought Fenton as he and his father continued on toward the ommissary. He wondered which dinosaur it would be. Then Fenton remembered something. Most of the dinosaurs that appeared in the scenes with human beings were going to be generated by computer animation and added in later. The only dinosaur that would actually be filmed *with* a human actor was the large mechanical carnotaurus, and that wasn't finished yet. That meant that Van would probably be filmed fighting an "imaginary" dinosaur, and that the dinosaur's image would be added later.

But if that was the case, why had Justin suggested that Fenton come watch them film this scene? It couldn't be that exciting just to see Van battle an imaginary creature. And what had Justin meant by "It should be a lot of fun"?

Suddenly Fenton thought he knew. It sounded a lot like Justin was planning one of his practical jokes, and Fenton wouldn't be surprised if it ended up being at Van's expense.

Fenton shook his head. If Justin didn't leave Van alone, Van might get so upset that he'd quit the movie. With everyone talking about all that had been going wrong with *Night of the Carnotaurus,* one more problem might be all Van needed to go over the edge.

Then Fenton had a thought. What if Justin somehow had a hand in some of the other things that had gone wrong as well? What if this supposed jinx everyone was talking about was really just the result of some of Justin Cho's practical jokes?

6

"Absolutely not!" yelled Van. "I can't work this way!"

"Van, Van," Ms. Cagney said soothingly. "Listen to me. All I'm saying is, let's give it a try. You can do that for us, can't you, Van?"

The film crew, along with Fenton and Justin, were out in a densely foliaged area behind one of the soundstage buildings.

"No!" said Van, shaking his head violently. "I told you, Constance, I cannot and I will not work without it!"

Ms. Cagney turned away from him and raised her voice. "Could we all please take one more look around for Mr. Steele's rabbit's foot? It's awfully important. Everybody, just look around. He says he had it in the pocket of his costume this morning, so it probably just fell out somewhere."

As Van began to frantically search the pockets of his futuristic-looking gray jumpsuit one more time, Fenton searched the grass. Fenton was looking, but he had the distinct feeling that the rabbit's foot hadn't fallen out of Van Steele's costume at all and that it wasn't going to be found that easily. Justin was crawling around on his hands and knees in the grass next to him, and once Fenton saw the grin on his face, he was more convinced than ever. Justin had definitely had something to do with this.

Tom Williams walked by, poking through the grass with the

toe of his work boot and shaking his head.

"Look, Van," said Ms. Cagney, "I have an idea. Why don't I send Tom out to get you a new rabbit's foot?"

"No!" said Van stubbornly. "I have to have *my* lucky rabbit's foot. I've had it with me for all of the movies I've ever made. And on this one I need it more than ever!"

"Now, Van," said Ms. Cagney in a warning tone, "let's not start that again."

"Don't try to cover it up, Constance," said Van. He looked around, a worried expression on his face. "This film is jinxed!"

Justin, still down on his hands and knees, began to snicker.

"Justin," whispered Fenton. "Did you take that rabbit's foot?"

Justin looked up, an expression of mock surprise on his face.

"Who, *me*?" he said. Then he broke into another grin. "Here, watch this," he whispered.

"Excuse me, Van," said Justin, standing up, "but are you sure you really checked all the pockets of your costume?"

"Of course I did," Van said miserably. "It's not there."

"Are you positive?" asked Justin again. He walked toward Van. "Because I thought I saw something sticking out back here."

He reached around to the back pocket of Van's jumpsuit.

"Why, here it is!" said Justin brightly. He lifted his hand. The small white rabbit's foot dangled from it.

"What?" said Van, a shocked expression on his face. "But I know I checked there! How could that be?"

"I have a funny feeling *I* know how," said Ms. Cagney in a tight voice. She looked pointedly at Justin.

Fenton sucked in his breath. Now Justin was sure to get it.

But just as Ms. Cagney was about to continue, Rosa Alvarez, the computer animator, arrived on the lot.

"Ms. Cagney, I have to talk to you," she said. "It's about the computer. I'm having some trouble with it again."

Ms. Cagney sighed and put her hand to her forehead.

"What is it now, Rosa?" she asked in a tired-sounding voice.

"I'm not sure, but it's acting awfully funny," said Rosa. "It's slowed down considerably. Whatever I ask it to do takes much longer than it ought to. Anyway, it means that those images you wanted by tomorrow aren't going to be ready."

A problem with the computer, thought Fenton. Could Justin possibly be responsible for that, too, somehow? He supposed it was possible that Justin could be some kind of computer whiz, like Max. Fenton looked around. Maybe if he could see how Justin was reacting to Rosa's news, that would give him a clue.

But Justin was nowhere to be found.

7

Late that night Fenton lay in his bed in the hotel room, tossing and turning. He could hear his father's deep, regular breathing in the other bed, but Fenton couldn't fall asleep. Finally he switched on the light and padded over to the mini-refrigerator, where he took out a small bottle of juice and a bag of pretzels.

Fenton climbed back into bed, took a sip of his juice, and bit into a pretzel. It was a good thing his father was a heavy sleeper. Fenton wished he could be sleeping too. But he had been going over various things in his mind—the incident with the rabbit's foot that day, the mistake in the drawing of the huayangosaurus, and Rosa's news about the computer—and he just couldn't seem to come to any conclusions. It didn't seem likely that Justin could be responsible for *everything* that had gone wrong with the movie, but Fenton couldn't be absolutely sure. He would just have to keep an eye on him.

And, as it turned out, Justin was the first person Fenton and his father saw the following morning. As they were entering the hotel restaurant for breakfast, Justin and a short, heavy-set, older woman were leaving.

"Hi, Fenton," said Justin. "This is my mom. Mom, this is Fenton, who I was telling you about."

"Hello, Fenton," said Justin's mother.

"Hi," said Fenton's father, reaching out to shake her hand. "I'm Bill Rumplemayer."

"Pleased to meet you," said Justin's mother.

"So," said Fenton, remembering his decision to try to keep an eye on Justin, "what are you doing today? I mean, are they shooting any more fun scenes?"

Justin smirked a little. "You mean like yesterday?" he said. "I hope so. I'm not in any of this morning's scenes, but we could go watch them film the rest of Van's big fight."

"Oh, no you don't," said Justin's mother.

Justin looked at her. "Why not?"

"Have you forgotten about your science report?" said his mother. "Mr. Twomble wants you to finish it by tomorrow. You'd better get to work on that this morning."

"Actually, Fenton," said Mr. Rumplemayer, "if I'm not mistaken, you have some schoolwork to do as well."

"Aw, Dad," said Fenton. What was his father thinking? This was no time to bring up homework.

"Galaxy has provided Justin with a trailer over by one of the lots so he can do his schoolwork on the set," said Justin's mother to Fenton's father. "You're welcome to have Fenton work there too, if you like."

"That sounds like a fine idea," said Mr. Rumplemayer. "I've got to go over to the computer-animation room and see if those new drawings for the huayangosaurus are ready anyway."

But it didn't sound like a fine idea to Fenton at all. The last thing he wanted to think about was school. And he wouldn't mind taking a look at the new huayangosaurus, either. But, he reminded himself, at least this way he'd be able to keep a close watch on Justin.

A little while later Fenton and Justin sat at a table in a corner of Justin's trailer, their schoolbooks spread out around them. Fenton looked down again at the list of vocabulary words. Today was Tuesday, which meant that Maggie had taken the vocabulary test yesterday. It was a little strange to think of Maggie and Willy back in Morgan, going to school and doing all their usual things while Fenton was out here in Hollywood. He certainly had a lot to tell them when he got home.

Fenton looked over at Justin, who was bent over a pad, apparently hard at work, his pencil scratching furiously against the paper.

Justin glanced up at him. "What do you think?" he asked, holding up his pad for Fenton to see.

On the pad was a detailed drawing of an eagle, its wings spread in flight.

"*That's* your homework?" Fenton said incredulously.

"No, of course not," said Justin. "It's a picture. Do you like it?"

Fenton had to admit it was a very good drawing. The eagle's beak was slightly open, and its toes were spread as if it was about to land. And there was a lot of detail; it looked as though Justin had drawn in every feather. Fenton thought of the stack of sketchbooks filled with his own dinosaur drawings in his room back in Morgan.

"It's really good," said Fenton. "I like to draw too."

"Yeah, well, anything's better than that stupid science report I'm supposed to do," said Justin.

"What are you doing it on?" asked Fenton.

Justin shrugged. "I can't think of anything."

"You should do it on dinosaurs," Fenton suggested.

"Nah, that's no fun," said Justin.

"Sure it is," said Fenton. "Dinosaurs were really cool."

"If they were so cool, why'd they all go extinct?" said Justin.

"Actually, a lot of scientists think it happened when a large asteroid hit the earth," said Fenton. "That it caused a huge dust cloud that blocked out the sun and made the earth's temperature go down."

"You mean they froze to death?" asked Justin, amazed.

"Or starved," said Fenton. "See, when the sun disappeared, it probably killed a lot of the plants, which meant the herbivore dinosaurs had nothing to eat. And once there were no herbivores, the carnivores who usually ate *them* starved."

"Oh, I get it," said Justin. "You know, I just always figured the dinosaurs all died off because they were big, slow peanut-brains."

"That's not true at all," said Fenton a little defensively. "A lot of the dinosaurs were probably very intelligent. Troodons had really big brains for their body size. And some dinosaurs were fast, too. Like the gallimimus. Scientists think it may have been able to run faster than twenty-five miles an hour."

"Wow," said Justin. "Somehow I can't imagine a big old dinosaur going that fast."

"Gallimimus were really lightly built, with long legs," explained Fenton. Then he had an idea. "Actually, there are some really good models of them upstairs in the model room."

"The model room seems like a pretty cool place," said Justin. "I used to hang out there, but then that Dr. Beech guy who was working up there said I couldn't anymore."

"Why not?" asked Fenton.

Justin grinned. "I guess it had something to do with the fact that I tied his shoelaces together while he was working."

Fenton shook his head. It seemed as if Justin would do anything for a laugh.

"Well, now my dad's in charge of the dinosaurs instead of him," he said. "So we can go look all we want. Besides," he added, "my dad wears loafers."

The two boys headed out of the trailer, and down Jupiter Lane to the technical building. On the way to the model room, Fenton poked his head into the computer-animation room across the hall. He saw his father working at a computer under some shelves, sitting next to a man wearing a baseball cap who was also working at a computer. Rosa was at another computer, on the other side of the room.

"Hi, Dad," said Fenton. "How's the huayangosaurus?"

Mr. Rumplemayer turned around. "Oh, hello, son, hello, Justin. Actually, we don't know yet. There seems to be some trouble with the computer, so the drawings aren't completed. Are you boys finished with your work?"

"Kind of," Fenton fibbed. "Anyway, I'm helping Justin with this report he's doing on dinosaurs, and I just want to show him something in the model-making room. I'll see you later."

"Okay, boys," said Mr. Rumplemayer, turning back to face the computer.

They walked into the model studio, where they saw Harry Brown, along with the woman Fenton had seen last time and another man, putting the finishing touches on some model hypsilophodons.

"Hi, there, Fenton," said Harry, looking up from his work. "Back for another visit? Oh, hi, Justin. No jokes today, I hope."

"Actually, we came up here to look at the gallimimus models," explained Fenton.

"Okay, sure," said Harry, getting back to work. "Go ahead, boys."

Fenton took Justin over to the shelves where the dinosaurs were assembled.

"Wow," said Justin, looking over the groups of figures. "These are amazing. I haven't been here since they finished all these. Are they all really dinosaurs?"

Fenton nodded. "Dinosaurs were really different from one another," he said. "There were over six hundred of them that we know about. And a new kind gets discovered about every seven weeks."

"That's incredible," said Justin.

"There," said Fenton, pointing to one of the long-necked, pointy-snouted dinosaurs on the shelf. "That's a gallimimus. See the long legs?"

"Yeah," said Justin. "It almost looks like an ostrich."

"Actually," said Fenton, "gallimimus is one of the ornithomimids, which a lot of people call the ostrich dinosaurs."

"Hey," said Justin, pointing to horned snout on one of the tiny bagaceratopses nearby, "this one's really funny-looking. What kind is it, Fenton?"

But Fenton didn't answer. He was busy looking at something else, a dinosaur on the next shelf. It was a dinosaur that he recognized, but something seemed very peculiar about it.

"Hold on," said Fenton, peering more closely at the new dinosaur. "There's something wrong with this ankylosaurid."

"This what?" said Justin.

"Ankylosaurid," said Fenton. "It's an armored dinosaur. And I think this one's supposed to be a euoplocephalus, from the Late Cretaceous. But it's missing its tail club."

"Its tail club?" Justin repeated.

"All the ankylosaurids have them," explained Fenton. "It's a bony knob on the ends of their tails. They may have used it for defense."

"That's pretty cool," said Justin. "But you say this ankylosaurid doesn't have one, huh? I wonder why not."

"Me too," said Fenton quietly, still studying the dinosaur.

Just then there was a huge crash from across the hall.

"What was that?" said Fenton and Justin, looking at each other.

"It sounds like something fell," said Harry Brown, looking alarmed.

Suddenly the young man Fenton had seen working at the computer by his father came rushing into the room.

"Help! Help!" he cried. "There's been an accident! Bill Rumplemayer is hurt!"

8

"Somebody get some ice!" said Rosa as Fenton, Justin, Harry, and the others rushed into the computer-animation room.

"I tell you, I'm fine," said Mr. Rumplemayer, who was standing in the middle of the room, looking dazed. He reached up to rub his head. "Ooch."

Fenton hurried over to his father. "What happened, Dad?"

"I don't know," said Mr. Rumplemayer. "I was working at the computer, and I felt something smash on my head."

"It was the shelf," said the man in the baseball cap. "I was sitting next to him, and I saw the whole thing happen. The shelf just suddenly came crashing down. It almost hit me, too."

Fenton looked over at the seat he had seen his father sitting in earlier. A set of shelves had been mounted to the wall above the seat, and the bottom one had come detached on one side. Scattered over the desk and on the floor were some books and papers, along with what appeared to be some stray pieces of metal and a few odds and ends of metal hardware—screws, coils, and the like.

"Oh, no!" said Rosa, hurrying over and crouching down on the floor. She picked up a few screws in her hand. "The saltasaurus D.I.D. was up on that shelf, and now it's ruined!" She shook her head. "This is going to set us back even more time."

Tom Williams came hurrying in and looked around.

"Oh my goodness," he said, looking very upset. "That shelf! Did she fall down right on top of you?"

Mr. Rumplemayer nodded, then winced a little.

"Gee," said Tom, wringing his hands. "That's just terrible."

"Dad," said Fenton, concerned, "maybe you ought to sit down or something."

"Here," said Justin, wheeling over one of the desk chairs.

Mr. Rumplemayersat down and rubbed his head again. Just then Constance Cagney came rushing into the room.

"Is everything okay?" she asked breathlessly. "I heard there'd been an accident." She hurried over to Fenton's father. "Oh, no! Mr. Rumplemayer, are you all right?"

"I think so," said Fenton's father. "My head hurts a bit, though."

"He took a heavy knock," said the man in the baseball cap.

"We have to get you to a doctor, then," said Ms. Cagney.

"No, really, that's not necessary," said Fenton's father. "In fact, I can probably get back to work in just a moment or two."

"Work? Oh, no, that's absolutely out of the question," said Ms. Cagney. "You are at the very least to take the rest of the day off to relax, Mr. Rumplemayer. I insist."

"Dad, that probably is a pretty good idea," agreed Fenton. "You should just go back to the hotel and take it easy."

"Well," said Mr. Rumplemayer, "I suppose a little time out might feel good right about now."

"Let me call a car for you," said Ms. Cagney.

"No, no," said Fenton's father. "The hotel's only down the

street. I can walk. Actually, I think a little air might do me good."

"I'll go with you, Dad," offered Fenton.

"I'd really prefer it if you took a car," said Ms. Cagney.

"No, no, I'm perfectly fine without one," said Mr. Rumplemayer. "And Fenton will be with me."

"All right," said Ms. Cagney. "But if there's anything I can get you, Mr. Rumplemayer, please don't hesitate to let me know."

"I will," said Mr. Rumplemayer. He turned to Fenton. "Come on, son, let's go."

"Okay, Dad," said Fenton. "Catch you later, Justin."

"Bye," Justin answered.

"Actually, Justin, I think I'd like to have a word with you right now," said Ms. Cagney. "Let's go over to my office together."

As Fenton helped his father out of the chair, he caught Justin's eye. Justin looked scared. And Fenton thought he knew why. Ms. Cagney obviously hadn't been too happy with Justin's behavior on the set lately. The fact that she wanted to talk to him in private couldn't be good news.

If only Justin hadn't insisted on pulling those pranks, thought Fenton. Ms. Cagney was obviously angry about the cat and the rabbit's foot. But the more Fenton thought about it now, the less likely he thought it was that Justin was responsible for everything that was going wrong on the set. Sure, he'd played a few pranks, but he wasn't out to ruin the whole movie. And changing the huayangosaurus's legs in the computer drawing just didn't seem like Justin's style. Although it was true that Justin was a very good artist, Fenton reminded himself.

But it did seem as though *someone* must be responsible for

everything that was going on. There had just been too many problems to call it coincidence. And the latest one had almost injured his father very badly.

Fenton turned to his father as they left the studio grounds and headed toward the Galaxy Hotel.

"Dad," he said, "don't you think it was pretty weird, the way the shelf just happened to come unattached from the wall and hit you on the head like that?"

"Weird? I don't know, son," said his father. "I'd probably use the word *painful.*"

"I know," said Fenton. "But what I mean is, doesn't it seem like there's an awful lot of stuff going wrong with this movie?"

"Well, I suppose making a movie is a complicated business," said Mr. Rumplemayer. "And with a film like this, where there are so many special effects, a few things are bound to go wrong."

"I guess," said Fenton. Then he thought of something. "Oh, there was another thing, too. A mistake with one of the dinosaurs. I noticed it in the model studio right before the accident."

"Another mistake?" said his father as they approached the hotel. "What do you mean?"

"It was with one of the models," said Fenton. "An ankylosaurid. It didn't have any tail club."

"Are you certain?" asked Mr. Rumplemayer.

"Positive," said Fenton. "It was sitting right there on the shelves with all the finished models. It looked just like a euoplocephalus, except that it was missing its tail club."

"That's odd," said his father as they walked into the hotel lobby. "I reviewed all the stop-action models yesterday, and I didn't notice anything like that. Well, I suppose I must have overlooked it. Did you point it out to anybody?"

Fenton shook his head. "I didn't get the chance."

"Well then, I should probably give Ms. Cagney a call at her office and let her know," said Fenton's father. "I wouldn't want anyone to put that faulty euoplocephalus in any of the scenes."

In the room, as his father made the phone call, Fenton went to the mini-refrigerator and took out a soda and a package of cheese and crackers. Sitting down on the bed, he began to think. He'd been at Galaxy Studios for only a couple of days, and already he'd discovered two incorrect dinosaurs. And then there'd been the problems with the computer, and now the shelf that had fallen on his father's head. Suddenly Fenton remembered something. Hadn't Dr. Beech, the first scientific advisor for the film, had to leave because of an accident? It was a little too coincidental that both of the film's dinosaur advisors, first Dr. Beech and now his father, had been the victims of accidents.

As his father hung up the phone, Fenton turned to him, so agitated that he almost spilled his soda all over the bed.

"Dad," he said, "I think you may be in danger."

"Danger? What are you talking about?" said his father, sitting on the bed a sigh. "I told you, I feel fine. I just need a little time to relax."

"No, I mean, I think somebody may be out to get you," said Fenton. "What I'm saying is, I think somebody may have loosened that shelf on purpose so it would fall on your head."

"Don't be silly, son," said his father. "It was an accident, that's all."

"No, really, Dad," Fenton insisted. "Think about it. Didn't Dr. Beech have to leave the movie because *he* had had an accident?"

"Well, yes, that's what I heard," said Mr. Rumplemayer. "But that doesn't mean anything. Besides, how could anyone possibly have known that I would be sitting in that chair under that shelf at that exact time?"

"I guess you've got a point," Fenton admitted. It was true that anyone who worked in the computer room could have been injured by the shelf. But Fenton still wasn't willing to give up the idea that someone might be up to no good.

"Anyway," his father went on, "what possible reason could anyone have for loosening that shelf?"

Fenton had to admit he didn't know. But he was going to do what he could to find out. And his first step would be taking a closer look at the shelf itself.

"Dad," he said, trying to sound casual, "I think I'm going to go take a walk around the studio grounds. You know, see if I can watch them filming any scenes or anything."

"That sounds like a good idea," said his father. "I'm probably going to rest a little, anyway. Just make sure you're not in anyone's way."

A few minutes later Fenton entered the Galaxy technical building and made his way upstairs to the computer-animation room. Rosa Alvarez was the only person in the room. As Fenton walked in the door, she looked up from her computer with an alarmed expression on her face.

"Oh, Fenton, it's you!" she said. "You startled me. I suppose I was just so involved in what I was doing . . ." Her voice trailed off.

"Where is everyone?" asked Fenton, looking around at the rows of unattended computers.

"Actually, I sent them home," said Rosa.

"Home?" Fenton repeated, eyeing the shelf that was still dangling above where his father had been sitting. Sending the computer animators home in the middle of the day when the movie was behind schedule certainly seemed like a strange thing to do.

"Yes," said Rosa. "We're having so much trouble with the computer that no one could get any work done anyway."

"What kind of trouble do you mean?" asked Fenton.

"Why?" asked Rosa quickly. "Do you know anything about computers?"

"Only a little," said Fenton.

"Well, this one seems to be operating at a fraction of its normal speed," said Rosa. "It's taking forever to get even the tiniest thing done."

Oh," said Fenton. He looked at the broken shelf again, trying to think of some excuse to go over and examine it.

Just then Tom Williams walked into the room, a dark blue metal tool chest in one hand.

"Oh, hello, Fenton," he said quietly. "How's your father feeling?"

"Okay, I guess," Fenton answered.

"I sure am glad to hear that," said Tom. "Terrible, what happened to him." He held up the tool chest. "Well, I'm here to fix that shelf."

"Oh, good. I was about to call you about that," said Rosa. She glanced at Fenton. "Fenton, can I help you with something? I mean, is there something you need here? Because, if not, I really need to get back to work now."

"Oh, okay," said Fenton. Too bad I missed my chance to look at that shelf, he added to himself as Tom began unpacking his tools.

Fenton made his way out of the computer-animation room and left the Galaxy Studios technical building. Outside on the street, he saw Justin coming toward him slowly, head hanging. In fact, Justin was so lost in whatever he was thinking about that he almost bumped right into Fenton.

"Hey, Justin, watch out," said Fenton.

Justin looked up, a worried expression on his face.

"Fenton, you've got to help me," he said. "Constance heard about the ankylosaurid, and she's convinced that I'm the one who damaged the model."

Fenton felt a pang. After all, he had been the one to notice the missing tail club in the first place. His father's call must have come right in the middle of Ms. Cagney's meeting with Justin.

"Well, I guess you have been pulling a lot of pranks," Fenton pointed out.

"I know, I know," said Justin. "And that's why she suspects me. But I'm not responsible for this one, or for *any* of the stuff that's gone wrong with the dinosaurs. I swear."

Fenton looked at Justin. Something in his new friend's face convinced him that Justin was telling the truth, that the trouble with the ankylosaurid wasn't just another one of Justin's practical jokes.

"You've got to believe me," said Justin miserably.

"I do believe you," Fenton told him.

There was no doubt about it—something strange was going on at Galaxy Studios. And it wasn't a jinx, either. No, someone was definitely up to no good on the set of *Night of the Carnotaurus*, someone who wanted to sabotage the movie. And Fenton was determined to figure out just who it was and why.

"Justin," he said, "we've got to come up with a plan."

"A plan?" said Justin.

"Yes" said Fenton. "Someone's trying to ruin this movie, and it's up to you and me to figure out who it is."

"But how are we supposed to do that?" asked Justin.

"I'm not sure," said Fenton, thinking. "But I do know that there's someone we should get in touch with right away. There are a couple of questions I'd like to ask him."

9

"I'd like to speak with Dr. Beech, please," said Fenton into the telephone. He turned to Justin. "Are you sure Ms. Cagney's not coming back to the office this afternoon?"

"Positive," said Justin. "She's directing Van and Kim on Soundstage Four all afternoon."

Fenton glanced nervously at the door. Justin had assured him that Ms. Cagney's office was the best place for them to make the call to Rupert College in Montana, since it had one of the few telephones that was private and that made long-distance calls.

A woman's voice picked up on the other end of the line. "Geology and Paleontology Department, may I help you?"

"Yes," said Fenton. "I'm trying to locate Dr. Beech."

"I'm sorry, but Dr. Beech isn't in," said the woman. "In fact, he won't be in for a few weeks."

"Oh," said Fenton. "Listen, do you think you could give me his home number? You see, it's really important, and—"

"But he can't be reached at home, either," said the woman, cutting him off. "Dr. Beech isn't in town."

"Oh," said Fenton, disappointed. He hung up. "Dr. Beech is out of town," he said to Justin. "Too bad. I really would have liked to ask him a few things about what was happening with the dinosaurs before he left. And I definitely wanted to find out more about his accident. You know, how and where it happened."

"It was in his hotel room," said Justin. "I just don't know how. But what does Dr. Beech's accident have to do with anything?"

"Don't you see?" said Fenton. "First Dr. Beech has an accident, and then my father, who's replacing him, has one too."

"Wow," said Justin, nodding. "You think maybe someone arranged both of those accidents?"

"That's right," said Fenton. "And I think whoever it was is responsible for the problems with the dinosaurs, too."

"But who?" asked Justin. "And why would they do it?"

"I don't know," said Fenton. He picked up a pad of paper from the desk. "Let's make a list of suspects."

"Just as long as I'm not on it, " said Justin, laughing.

"I did kind of suspect you a little at first," admitted Fenton.

"Oh, come on," said Justin. "Why would I want to ruin the dinosaurs for the movie? Besides, even if I did want to, I wouldn't know how to do all that stuff with the computer and everything."

"But I know someone who would," said Fenton. "Rosa Alvarez." He wrote her name down on the pad.

"You mean the woman in the computer room?" asked Justin.

Fenton nodded. "She's a computer-animation specialist."

"But why would she want to ruin a movie that she's working on?" asked Justin.

Fenton thought a moment. "In order to keep her job longer," he said finally. "Rosa told me and my dad that she gets hired for only one movie at a time," he explained. "So as long as this movie goes on, she's got a job. Maybe she started messing up some of the dinosaur stuff just so the movie would be delayed more."

"That makes sense," said Justin, nodding.

"In fact," said Fenton, "today she told me she sent all the animators home. And she looked really startled when I walked in the room. Maybe she was in the middle of changing another dinosaur." He thought again. "And then there's Harry Brown, the dinosaur-model maker."

"Why him?" asked Justin.

"For one thing," said Fenton, "he just started working here. Before this he worked for some studio called Worldwide."

"Wow, Worldwide and Galaxy are big rivals!" said Justin.

"That's what I heard," said Fenton. "So I figure maybe Harry's *still* working for Worldwide—as a spy."

"Sure," said Justin. "*Night of the Carnotaurus* is one of Galaxy's biggest films this year. Worldwide would definitely be happy if the movie never got finished."

Fenton wrote down Harry Brown's name on the pad too.

"Now, who else . . ." he began, thinking again.

Just then Fenton heard a noise outside the door to the office.

"What was that?" he said to Justin.

"Someone's coming!" said Justin.

"I thought you said Ms. Cagney was directing all afternoon," Fenton whispered.

"That's what she said," Justin hissed back.

There was a click, and the doorknob began to turn.

"Quick! Hide somewhere!" said Fenton, looking wildly around the office.

But it was too late. The door was already opening.

10

"What are you boys doing in here?"

Fenton sighed in relief. It wasn't Ms. Cagney, only Tom.

"We, uh, I forgot something in here earlier when I was talking to Constance," Justin blurted out. He grabbed the pad from Fenton's hand. "Oh, there it is. Good. Okay, Fenton, I guess we can go now."

"Yeah, I guess so," said Fenton. "See you, Tom."

"Bye, Tom!" added Justin as they hurried out the door.

"Phew," said Fenton when they got downstairs, "that was close. We could have been in real trouble."

"Could have?" said Justin. "Fenton, we *are* in trouble. Or I am, at least. Tom's sure to tell Constance we were in her office, and she'll think I was up to something again." He moaned. "Oh, why did I have to play all those stupid practical jokes to begin with?"

"Don't worry, Justin," said Fenton. "Ms. Cagney will find out soon enough that you're not the one sabotaging the movie—just as soon as we figure out who is."

"I hope you're right," said Justin.

"So, Dad," said Fenton the next day over lunch in the hotel restaurant, "how much do you know about Dr. Beech's accident?"

"Nothing, really, son," Mr. Rumplemayer answered. He took a sip of his coffee.

"You know that he broke his leg, right?" Fenton prompted.

"Yes, I believe that's what I heard," said his father, taking a bite of his sandwich.

"So then, maybe you should ask someone how it happened," suggested Fenton. "Like Ms. Cagney or someone. I mean, you know, just so you could find out for sure."

"Fenton," said Mr. Rumplemayer impatiently, "I know what you're getting at, and I want you to forget it. As I told you before, there's absolutely no connection between whatever happened to Dr. Beech and that shelf that fell down."

"But Dad—" Fenton began.

"Fenton, that's enough," said Mr. Rumplemayer sharply. "Please remember that I'm here to do a job. Ms. Cagney has been very generous in allowing you to come too, and I hope you won't let your wild imaginings jeopardize our position here."

"Okay, Dad," said Fenton in a low voice.

But Fenton knew that if he didn't figure out what was happening soon, more than their position at Galaxy could be jeopardized. If only he had been able to reach Dr. Beech in Montana! Why did Dr. Beech have to be out of town?

Suddenly Fenton thought of something. Dr. Beech had supposedly gone out of town, but he'd broken his leg only a couple of weeks earlier. Who would go out of town with a broken leg? There was definitely something very strange about that. Fenton decided to find Justin right away so they could talk about it.

"Dad, I've got to go," said Fenton, gulping down the last of his chocolate milk. “I just remembered that Justin said I should stop by the soundstage where they’re shooting now.”

“I thought you wanted to go to the technical building with me this afternoon,” said his father.

“I do,” said Fenton. “But I just have to stop by and see Justin first. I’ll meet you there in a little while, okay?”

“All right,” said Mr. Rumplemayer. “I’ll be reviewing Rosa’s reconstruction of the saltasaurus D.I.D. first, and then later I’ll be in the south wing, looking at the mechanical carnotaurus.”

“Okay, I’ll catch up with you later,” said Fenton.

Fenton found Justin on Soundstage 3, sitting astride a large cylindrical pipe between Van and Kim. The pipe was suspended several feet in the air, supported on either end by metal brackets, and behind the actors was a bright blue screen. The scene didn’t make much sense to Fenton, but that was the last thing on his mind at the moment.

Between takes, Fenton tried to get Justin’s attention. The lights trained on the actors were very bright, though, and Fenton realized that Justin probably couldn’t see beyond the cameras.

Finally Ms. Cagney called a break. Someone brought over a step stool, and the actors climbed down from the pipe and made their way through the maze of lights and cameras. Suddenly Van stopped short.

“Who left that there?” he demanded, pointing at a large ladder directly in his path.

Ms. Cagney hurried over.

“Van, Van, calm down now,” she said in a soothing voice. “It’s just a ladder.”

"*Just* a ladder?" Van repeated incredulously. "*Just* a ladder? Do you know how close I just came to walking right under that thing?" He ran his hand nervously through his hair. "Ladders are very bad luck, Constance."

"All right, all right," said Ms. Cagney. "We'll have someone move it right away. Just calm down, Van." She looked around. "Tom, could you get someone to move that ladder please? Where is he? Could somebody move that ladder away from Mr. Steele?"

A red-haired man in jeans came hurrying over and moved the ladder out of the way.

Fenton caught Justin's eye and motioned him over.

"Hi," said Justin. "Boy, Van's been about to lose his mind all day." He glanced back at the pipe and the blue screen. "That's supposed to be the scene where we're riding on the back of that big dinosaur. I think it's called a salt-something."

"Saltasaurus," Fenton corrected.

"Yeah, saltasaurus, that's it," said Justin. "For now we're just riding on that dumb pipe, but they're going to add the dinosaur and the background later."

"Oh," said Fenton. "Listen, Justin, we need to find out about Dr. Beech's accident."

"I already told you," said Justin. "It happened in his hotel room. Why? Did something else happen to your dad?"

"No, but I thought of something. The woman who answered the phone at Dr. Beech's college said he'd gone out of town."

"So?" said Justin.

"So don't you think that's a little strange?" asked Fenton.

"I don't know," said Justin, shrugging. "What's so strange

about going out of town?"

"Nothing," said Fenton. "That is, unless you're doing it with a broken leg."

"Wow," said Justin. "You're right. What do you think it means, Fenton?"

"Well, either he's not really out of town, or he didn't really break his leg," said Fenton. "Or both. Listen, I have to go meet my dad in the technical building now. Do you think you can get into Ms. Cagney's office again today?"

"I guess so," said Justin. "She's shooting a scene after this one with Kim and Van that I'm not in. Why?"

"Because," said Fenton, "I want you to make another call to Rupert College."

A little while later Fenton walked into the technical building and pressed the button for the elevator. When the elevator door opened, his father and Rosa Alvarez came out.

"Oh, hello, Fenton," said Rosa.

"Hi," said Fenton, eyeing her. "Where are you going?"

"Son," Mr. Rumplemayer chided, "that's a little rude."

Rosa laughed. "That's okay," she said. "Actually, I'm leaving early. The computer is still operating at a snail's pace, so there isn't much anyone can do here now. Besides, I was here late last night rebuilding that saltasaurus D.I.D., and now that your father says it checks out okay, I think I'll go catch up on some rest."

"You're just in time to go over to the south wing with me and take a look at that carnotaurus, though, if you want, Fenton," said his father. "I hear they've got it just about finished."

"Okay," said Fenton. He was looking forward to seeing the completed model. Besides, he thought, it might be a good idea to do some snooping around the south wing while he was there.

Fenton and his father made their way through the maze of hallways toward the south wing. As they turned the final corner, they practically bumped into Harry Brown, who was exiting the construction area.

"Oh, hello," said Harry, looking startled.

"Hi," said Fenton's father. "Looks like you're coming from where we're headed. How are they coming on the carnotaurus?"

"Um, pretty well, I guess," said Harry. "I just went in to take a peek at it, really." He glanced around quickly. "I suppose I'd better get back upstairs to the model room, though. Ms. Cagney probably wouldn't be too pleased to see me wandering around when there's work to do and we're so behind schedule already."

That's for sure, thought Fenton, eyeing him suspiciously.

Harry hurried away, and Fenton and his father entered the construction area, where they saw the huge carnotaurus model, which was nearly completed now. Its tail was covered in scaly skin, and the short, stubby forearms had been attached to the body.

"Well, I'd say it's pretty convincing," said Mr. Rumplemayer, gazing up at the huge creature.

"That's for sure," agreed Fenton. If he hadn't known better, he would have thought he was standing beneath a genuine carnotaurus.

"You should see it when it's moving," said a voice.

Fenton turned and saw a short man with a brown beard.

"You folks must be the Rumplemayers," said the man. "The

name's Stolp. Fred Stolp, but everybody just calls me Stolp. I'm the dinosaur wrangler."

"Wrangler?" said Fenton.

"Sure," said Stolp with a grin. "I'm the one who makes it move." He shook hands with Fenton's father. "I'm the chief engineer here. I suppose you're the one Ms. Cagney sent to check up on how I've done."

"Well, you could put it that way . . ." Fenton's father began.

"And so I did!" said Stolp, chuckling. "So, how about I give you folks a little demonstration?" He turned to Fenton. "What do you say there, young fella? Care to take a little ride?"

"A ride?" said Fenton. "Oh, you mean inside the carnotaurus? You bet! Can I, Dad?"

"If Mr. Stolp says so," said his father.

Fenton followed Stolp over to the ladder that led up to the open hatchway in the carnotaurus's chest.

As they climbed up the ladder, Stolp turned to him. "Now, you have a valid dinosaur-driver's license, don't you, young fella?"

Fenton laughed. Stolp was pretty funny. He almost made Fenton forget about all the bad things that had been happening around the studio.

As they climbed inside the dinosaur, Fenton looked around. They were in a small area with two seats. On either side of each seat were several levers.

"This almost looks like the cockpit of a plane," said Fenton.

"So it does," agreed Stolp. "Now, which do you want to control, the arms and head, or the legs?"

Fenton thought a moment. "The arms and head," he decided.

"Okay then, you sit over here," said Stolp, indicating the seat on the left.

As Fenton sat down, he realized that there were tiny, mesh-covered windows set into the dinosaur's chest, and that he had a pretty good view of the room in front of him. Stolp settled into the other seat.

"Now, these over here make the arms move," Stolp explained, pointing to the two levers to Fenton's left. "Go ahead, give them a try."

Fenton pulled on one of the levers. He heard a mechanical-sounding creak somewhere above him.

"There you go," said Stolp. "You just made the old guy wave hello. The lever on your right makes the mouth open and close. Go ahead, give it a try."

Fenton practiced with the different levers for a moment, making the dinosaur's arms and mouth move.

"Okay, now we're going to take this old guy for a little stroll," said Stolp. He reached for his own levers, and suddenly Fenton felt the carnotaurus lurch forward. "Here we go!" said Stolp. "Now, don't forget to do your part, so we can give your dad a good show."

For another minute or so, Fenton and Stolp operated their levers, putting the dinosaur into motion and making it take a couple more steps.

"Wow, this is fun," said Fenton. Wait until he told Maggie and Willy that he had driven a dinosaur. They would never believe it.

"Okay, copilot, we better stop now before we walk through a wall," said Stolp. "Let's find out how your dad liked the show."

Fenton and Stolp descended from the carnotaurus. Mr. Rumplemayer was standing nearby, looking up at the dinosaur, his arms folded across his chest.

"I'm very impressed," said Mr. Rumplemayer. "That was extremely lifelike. In fact, it didn't appear mechanical at all."

"That was me doing the arms and the mouth, Dad," said Fenton proudly.

"Well then, do we get your seal of approval?" asked Stolp.

"Without a doubt," said Fenton's father. "I'd say you couldn't have done a better job with this carnotaurus."

Fenton was pleased. It was nice to know that something had finally gone well with one of the movie's dinosaurs.

Just then Fenton saw Justin poke his head into the room and beckon to him.

"I'll see you later, Dad," said Fenton. "I'm going to hang around with Justin for a while. Maybe we'll do some homework in his trailer," he added for good measure.

"All right, son," said his father. "Just make sure you're back at the hotel for dinner in a little while."

"Okay," called Fenton, jogging toward Justin. "Oh, and thanks for the ride, Stolp."

"No problem at all, young fella," said Stolp. "You're a terrific driver."

Fenton made his way out into the hall, where he found Justin waiting for him.

"Hi, Justin," he said. "What's up? Did you make that call?"

"I sure did," said Justin. "And wait till you hear this. You were right—Dr. Beech never went back to Montana at all. The woman who answered the phone said he was in California, *working on a movie.*"

"Wow," said Fenton. "So it's true."

"What's true?" asked Justin. "I don't get it, Fenton. Why did you have me make that call, and what does it mean?"

"Don't you see?" said Fenton. "Dr. Beech is the culprit. He's the one who's been sabotaging the movie."

"He has?" said Justin. "How do you know?"

"Think about it," said Fenton. "He supposedly broke his leg, but he did it in his hotel room where no one could see it. Then he says he's leaving the set of the movie because of his accident, but he doesn't even go home to Montana."

"I guess it is sort of suspicious," said Justin.

"Of course it is," said Fenton. "The way I see it, Dr. Beech did all he could to sabotage the dinosaurs while he was working on the movie. But then someone must have gotten onto him or something, so he came up with the broken leg excuse to leave the set. That way no one would be able to blame it on him."

"But how come things keep happening now that he's gone?" asked Justin.

"Maybe he's sneaking in at night or something," said Fenton. "He could easily have made a copy of the keys to the technical building before he left."

"That's true," said Justin. "But now what do we do? We can't just march into Constance's office and announce that Dr. Beech is the one responsible for everything. She'd never believe us."

"That's why we have to get proof," said Fenton. "And I have a pretty good idea where we should start."

11

"Are you sure no one is in there?" asked Justin as he and Fenton peered around the corner of the hallway at the closed door of the computer-animation room.

"Positive," said Fenton. "I saw Rosa leave. No one could do any more work because the computer was so messed up."

"Gosh, what do you think's wrong with it?" asked Justin.

"I don't know," said Fenton. "But it's one of the things I want to try to find out. Come on, let's go."

They hurried to the computer-animation room.

"Wait," said Fenton as Justin reached for the light switch. He pointed to the small window in the door. "Someone might see."

Fenton reached down behind the nearest computer terminal and switched it on. Soon all the computers were on, and the darkened room was filled with an eerie green glow.

"Now what do we do?" said Justin, looking around the room.

"I don't know," said Fenton. Then he thought of something. "But I bet I know who does." He sat down in front of a computer. "Now, if I can only find the modem program on this thing."

"Modem?" said Justin. "Are you going to call someone?"

"Yeah," said Fenton. "If I can." He glanced at his watch. Four thirty. Seven thirty New York time. Hopefully Max would be in front of his computer. Fenton highlighted the options on the computer's menu and located the modem program. "Here goes," he said, keying in Max's number, along with a quick message.

"My friend Max in New York knows all about computers," Fenton explained. "I sure hope he'll be able to figure out what's going on with this one." He glanced down at the screen. "Boy, Rosa was right, this thing *is* taking forever."

Just then Fenton noticed a robotic figure on the desk nearby.

"I guess this is the rebuilt saltasaurus D.I.D.," he said, examining the metal model. He moved one of the dinosaur's legs a little.

"Looks pretty cool," said Justin.

"Yeah," said Fenton. Then he noticed something strange about the model's tail. "Hey," he said, "this is weird."

"What?" asked Justin.

"This tail is stiff," said Fenton. "Saltasaurus was unusual because it had a flexible tail. Scientists think their tails might have been able to brace them when they reared back to eat."

"Wow," said Justin. "Another dinosaur mistake."

"This one's definitely not a mistake," said Fenton, running his finger along the saltasaurus's tail joints. "My father checked this dinosaur out earlier today, and I know he never would have missed something like this."

"Are you sure?" asked Justin. "I mean, he is still getting over that bump on the head."

"I'm positive," said Fenton. "My father would have noticed this blindfolded. Somebody deliberately fused this tail joint together after my father looked at it."

"Hey," said Justin suddenly, pointing at the computer screen.

"Someone's answering."

Fenton looked down at the screen. There was the response.

<**IS THAT U? I THOUGHT U WERE IN HOLLYWOOD**>

"It's Max!" said Fenton happily. He keyed in his response.

]I AM. I AM AT GALAXY STUDIOS RIGHT NOW[

<**WOW. WHATS IT LIKE?**>

]KIND OF STRANGE. I DONT HAVE TIME TO EXPLAIN, BUT
I NEED YOUR HELP WITH SOME COMPUTER STUFF[

Fenton quickly described the problems Rosa Alvarez had said she was having with the computer, how it had been taking much longer than it should to do even the simplest tasks.

<**SOUNDS LIKE THE COMPUTERS BEEN OVERLOADED**>

Max anwered.

Fenton and Justin looked at each other.

"Ask him what he means," said Justin.

]WHAT DO U MEAN BY THAT?[

Fenton keyed in.

<**A COMPUTER CAN SLOW DOWN BECAUSE SOMETHING ELSE IS DRAINING IT. IF ITS BEEN PROGRAMMED 2 DO SOME REALLY BIG JOB OF SOME KIND**>

Fenton looked at the screen and froze. Suddenly he thought he knew just what that big job might be.

"The dinosaurs!" he and Justin said at once.

With Max's help, Fenton and Justin checked out the graphics program on the computer. Sure enough, someone had instructed the computer to change just about every one of the dinosaurs, but to do it so slowly that no one would even notice that it was taking place. And the most amazing part of all was that the dinosaur "mistakes" that Fenton had spotted in other places were here in the computer, too. The euoplocephalus was missing its tail club, and the saltasaurus's tail was completely stiff. Even the huayangosaurus's front legs, which had supposedly been corrected, were back to their original incorrect length. *This* must be the huge job that was draining the computer's resources!

<MAYBE THE WORK OF SOME KIND OF HACKER>

Max commented.

]U MEAN WORKING FROM ANOTHER COMPUTER?[

Fenton asked him.

<SURE, IF THEY HAD A MODEM. IT PROBABLY WOULDNT BE THAT HARD 2 FIGURE OUT HOW 2 GET INTO THE DINO GRAPHICS PROGRAM + CHANGE IT>

]OK, I GET IT. THANKS 4 THE HELP[

<NO PROB. MODEM ME WHEN U GET BACK 2 MORGAN + TELL ME WHAT HAPPENS>

]OK. TALK 2 U THEN[

As Fenton signed off, he glanced at his watch.

"Wow," he said. "It's almost six o'clock. I'd better get back to the hotel to meet my dad."

"I've got to go too," said Justin. "I'm supposed to have a math class with Mr. Twomble."

"Math?" said Fenton incredulously. "At six o'clock at night?"

Justin shrugged. "He's a tutor. It's not like regular school."

"I'll say," said Fenton. "That makes regular school sound like Christmas vacation. Come on, let's go."

They shut off the computers and opened the door.

"Gee," said Fenton as they walked out into the dark, deserted hallway, "I guess everyone left."

"Yeah," said Justin softly. "Hey, Fenton, do you still think it was Dr. Beech sneaking in here at night who did all this stuff?"

"I don't know," said Fenton as they inched their way down the dark hall. "According to Max, the computer part could have been done from just about anywhere. One thing I do know. Whoever's been sabotaging the dinosaurs is waiting until after my dad has inspected them first. The thing with the ankylosaurid's tail club happened the day after my father had looked at all the models. And the saltasaurus's tail must have been done pretty recently, since he examined the D.I.D. today. And the trouble with the computer started right *after* my father had approved all the animation images."

"It's like there's a pattern," said Justin when they got downstairs. "Maybe we can figure out what'll be tampered with next."

Fenton stopped in his tracks. Justin was right. There *was* a pattern. And suddenly Fenton had no doubt at all about which dinosaur would be next.

12

"Don't you see?" Fenton said to Justin as they stood in the darkened lobby of the technical building. "It's got to be the mechanical carnotaurus! My father looked it over today."

"But it's huge," said Justin. "How could anyone get away with doing anything to it? They'd be noticed right away."

"I know," said Fenton, nodding. "Which is why I'm almost positive that they'll try to do it at night. And my guess is that it'll happen soon, maybe even tonight."

"That makes sense," agreed Justin. "So, what do you think we should do? Tell Constance?"

"Not yet," said Fenton. "She probably wouldn't believe us. And anyway, we don't know for sure that it'll happen tonight."

Fenton pushed open the front door of the building.

"I have another idea," said Fenton, reaching into his jean jacket pocket and taking out *The Pocket Book of One Thousand Interesting Dinosaur Facts.* He wedged the small paperback book between the door and the frame to keep it from latching shut. "There," he said, smiling at Justin. "Now we can get back in."

An hour later Fenton sat with his father in the hotel restaurant, wolfing down his mashed potatoes in giant spoonfuls.

"Dad," he managed to say, his mouth still full of potatoes, "can I go now? I promised Justin I'd be there right after dinner."

"Hold on," said his father. "It's wonderful that you and Justin are so eager to get started on your schoolwork, but I'm sure he can wait until you swallow your food."

Fenton gulped down the potatoes as a waiter approached. He and Justin had to be back at the technical building soon if his plan was going to work.

"Dessert?" said the waiter.

"No," said Fenton quickly. "Dad, can I go?"

"All right, all right," said Mr. Rumplemayer. "You certainly are eager this evening, Fenton. I hope you keep up this new enthusiasm for your schoolwork when we get back to Morgan."

But Fenton didn't answer. He was halfway to the door.

"Okay now, wait, explain this again," said Justin as they wandered through the darkened halls of the technical building toward the south wing. "What's all this stuff about a horse?"

"The Trojan horse," said Fenton, stuffing his paperback into his jacket pocket. "It happened in ancient Greece. My friend Maggie told me all about it. The Greeks were at war, and they needed to figure out a way to get inside the walls of the city of Troy, so they hid all their soldiers inside this statue of a horse on wheels."

"So you figure we can use the carnotaurus as a sort of Trojan dinosaur," said Justin.

"Exactly," said Fenton. "The carnotaurus is the perfect place for us to hide. If anyone tries to do anything to it, we're sure to spot them."

The two boys entered the enormous darkened room. Moonlight streamed through the windows of the giant garage-style door, and the carnotaurus, standing motionless, looked more real than ever, almost as though it was about to start moving.

"Wow," said Justin in awe. "This is really something."

"It moves, too," said Fenton. "I got to work the arms and the mouth. Come on, I'll show you how to get in."

They climbed up the ladder and through the hatch door in the dinosaur's chest.

"This is so cool," said Justin, settling into the seat on the left.

"I know. Isn't it?" agreed Fenton, taking the other seat.

"So tell me more about this carnotaurus," said Justin.

"Well," Fenton began, "you can't really see them that well right now because it's so dark, but there are all these levers here that control the various parts—"

"No," said Justin. "I mean the *real* carnotaurus. Maybe I'll write something about it for my science report."

"Oh, okay," said Fenton. "Carnotaurus lived at the beginning of the late Cretaceous, about 91 to 113 million years ago."

"Is that when most of the dinosaurs lived?" asked Justin.

"Actually, they lived anywhere from 65 to 230 million years ago," Fenton explained. "The Cretaceous was the end of the age of dinosaurs, after the Triassic and the Jurassic. Scientists aren't sure what the horns were for, but they think they might have been used for display. You know, to impress other carnotauruses."

"You mean they weren't for fighting?" asked Justin.

"Probably not," Fenton answered. "A big carnivore like this one wouldn't need a weapon like that. Its teeth were all it

needed—although it couldn't have been able to do much with those stubby arms. That's kind of the interesting thing about dinosaurs like carnotaurus and T. rex—"

"Hold on," Justin said suddenly. "Did you see that?"

A small beam of light passed over the mesh-covered windows in the dinosaur's chest.

"It looks like it's coming from outside," hissed Fenton.

"What do we do?" asked Justin.

"Just stay put," said Fenton. "And let them come to us."

The beam of light passed over the windows a couple more times. Fenton felt his stomach tightening. Ever since he'd arrived at Galaxy, he'd wanted nothing more than to catch whoever was sabotaging the movie, but now that it was about to happen, he couldn't help feeling a little scared.

Fenton heard a low rumble, followed by a long creaking sound.

"Hey," he whispered to Justin, realizing what he had heard, "I think someone's opening that big door."

Justin leaned forward to peer out the mesh-covered windows.

"Not only that," he said softly, "but they're backing in some kind of giant truck."

Fenton could hear the rumble of the truck's engine and smell the exhaust. Why would someone be bringing a truck in here, he thought. This wasn't what he had been expecting at all. Then suddenly he had a thought.

He turned to Justin in a panic. "Quick," said Fenton. "We've got to get out of here."

But it was too late. The big carnotaurus was already moving.

13

"Where are we going?" asked Justin as the truck with the carnotaurus inside rumbled along.

"I wish I knew," said Fenton uneasily. He thought of his father, who was back at the hotel, and who assumed that Fenton was safe in Justin's trailer, doing his homework. If anything happened to them, his father and Justin's mother wouldn't even know where to look. Suddenly this whole Trojan-dinosaur thing didn't seem like a very good idea after all.

If only I could see outside, Fenton thought as the truck drove along. Then he remembered the maze of highway exits and billboards he and his father had passed on the way to the movie studio from the airport. Even if he could see outside, he realized, he still probably wouldn't have any idea where they were headed.

A few minutes later the truck slowed down, made a few turns, and finally came to a stop. Fenton heard the doors to the truck's cab open and close, and men's voices talking.

He leaned toward Justin. "Let's just sit tight and see what happens," he whispered in Justin's ear.

"You got it," Justin whispered back.

The back door to the truck was opened and some light filtered in through the mesh-covered windows. Fenton and Justin gripped their seats as the big carnotaurus began to be slowly backed out of the truck.

"Watch it there! Watch it!" said one of the men's voices. "Take it out carefully, you hear?"

"Yeah," said another voice. "Watch out there, boys. Mitchell says he doesn't want a single scratch on this baby, you hear?"

"Mitchell?" whispered Justin softly. "Who's that?"

Fenton shrugged. He leaned forward to look out the window, but all he could see was what looked like a dark green wall moving toward them.

"Let's push it up over this way," said the first voice as the dinosaur continued to move toward the wall in tiny increments.

As the wall blocked out the window, it grew darker inside the carnotaurus. Finally the dinosaur came to a stop.

"That's it," said another man, whose voice sounded vaguely familiar to Fenton. "Let's just leave her right there."

"Okay, fine," said one of the other men. "Let's go tell Mitchell and the rest of them we've got it."

There were footsteps as the men walked away.

Fenton waited a few moments for the sounds to fade before turning to Justin. "Come on. Let's get out of here and try and find out where we are."

The boys reached over to open the hatch door in the dinosaur's chest, but it wouldn't budge.

"Uh-oh," said Justin, giving the door another shove. "It looks like we're stuck in here."

"The door must be wedged up against the wall," said Fenton. He thought a moment. "There's only one thing we can do."

He looked down at the levers near his seat. If only he had told Stolp that he wanted to learn to operate the carnotaurus's legs, instead of its arms and its mouth. Well, he'd just have to figure out how to make the creature take a step or two backward.

Fenton reached for the lever to his right and pulled it toward him. There was a mechanical whirring, and a large thud as one of the carnotaurus's feet kicked the wall in front of them.

"Oops," said Fenton.

"Are you crazy?" said Justin. "What if they come back?"

"It's a chance we have to take," said Fenton. "Right now it's our only hope of getting out of this thing."

He grabbed the lever again, this time pushing it forward. Sure enough, the carnotaurus shifted away from the wall slightly.

"One more step ought to do it," said Fenton. He took hold of the other lever, the one to his left, and pushed it, backing the carnotaurus away from the wall a full step.

"Nice work," said Justin, reaching out to pop open the hatch.

The boys crawled out of the hatch and dropped to the floor. They were in some sort of large warehouse. The walls were all painted green, and there were boxes stacked everywhere. Each box was marked in green with a picture of a globe supported by a pair of *W*s. The globe-and-*W*s insignia was painted on one of the walls, as well.

"Oh my gosh!" said Justin. "I know where we are. This is Worldwide Studios."

"You mean where Harry Brown used to work?" asked Fenton.

"That's right," said Justin. "Galaxy's biggest rival. 'Mitchell' must be Nathan Mitchell, the head of Worldwide. Wow, Fenton, I guess maybe you were right about Harry. Maybe he is a spy."

"Maybe," said Fenton. "Come on, let's try to get out of here. All we have to do now is call Galaxy and tell someone there where the carnotaurus is."

"Boy, Constance'll have to believe me when she hears this," said Justin.

Just then Fenton heard voices.

"Hold on," he said. "I think someone's coming."

The two boys ducked down behind a stack of boxes as the voices grew louder. Fenton recognized one of the voices from before; it was the first man he had heard speaking when the carnotaurus was being unloaded.

"All right, Doc, just be do what you're told and there won't be any trouble," said the man gruffly.

"Please, can't I go now?" said a second man's voice. "I've done everything that you've asked me. Couldn't you please let me go?"

"That's up to Mitchell," said the first man. "We're not through with you until he says we're through."

Fenton peered through a crack between two boxes. He saw an older, white-haired man in a rumpled suit. The man's hands were behind his back, and he was being pushed along by another, younger man.

"Please," said the older man, "all I ask is that you let me go back to Montana."

Fenton and Justin shot each other a wild look, and Fenton moved out of the way to let Justin take a peek. Justin looked back at Fenton and nodded.

"It's him," he whispered. "It's Dr. Beech."

"You'll go when Mr. Mitchell says you can go," said the younger man. "He's got one more dinosaur he wants you to 'fix' first."

"But surely you must realize that my colleagues at Rupert will be wondering were I am?" said Dr. Beech in a trembling voice.

"Don't you worry about your buddies back there at the college, old-timer," said the younger man. "Mr. Mitchell can come up with something to satisfy them. Just like he did with that lady director." He laughed. "Calling her up and telling her he was your doctor, treating you for a broken leg. She bought that story hook, line, and sinker!"

So, thought Fenton, Dr. Beech hadn't broken his leg after all! But he wasn't the one who was sabotaging the film, either. At least, not of his own free will. The broken-leg story must have been something that the thugs from Worldwide had come up with so they could kidnap Dr. Beech and force him to use his scientific knowledge to help them ruin the film. But if Dr. Beech had been held captive here at Worldwide for the past couple of weeks, who had been tampering with the models and things over at Galaxy?

There was no time to think about it, though. Dr. Beech and his captor had moved on; this was Fenton and Justin's chance.

"Come on," said Fenton. "Quick. Let's go before someone else comes and sees us."

"Over there," said Justin, pointing to what looked like a hallway a few yards away. "Maybe there's a way out."

The boys crept out from behind the boxes and hurried down the hall. There were several doors on each side of it, and Fenton felt sure that one of them would open any moment. He could feel his heart pounding with fear. It was clear from the way these people were treating Dr. Beech that they were serious about what they were doing. Fenton was sure they wouldn't be very happy to discover that he and Justin were sneaking around.

Suddenly they came upon an open door. Beyond it was a small office with a desk and a telephone.

"Look," said Justin, pointing. "We can call Galaxy."

"No, Justin, don't do it," said Fenton, backing away. "Someone could come any minute."

"It might be the only chance we get," said Justin. "Don't worry, I'll be really quick." He darted into the office and gently shut the door behind him.

Fenton stood outside the door, fidgeting nervously. He definitely didn't think it was a good idea for Justin to be in that office. He wandered down to the end of the hall and peered around. The coast seemed clear, but what was taking Justin so long? Fenton walked back to the other end of the hall, toward the warehouse itself. As he did, he heard voices from behind one of the doors. He looked around wildly, but there was nowhere to go. The voices were between him and the office that Justin was in.

Fenton sprinted back into the warehouse and slid behind a stack of boxes. He heard a door open and the voices coming down the hall. He crossed his fingers and hoped that Justin wouldn't choose that moment to come out of the office.

The first voice Fenton heard was a new one, one he hadn't heard before. It was a man.

"Now, just what seems to be the problem here?" he said. "You're going to get everything you were promised. The money, a new job. I don't see what you're complaining about."

The next man to speak was the one whose voice had seemed so familiar to Fenton. It was older sounding, and a bit raspy.

"But Mr. Mitchell," he said, "the way I heard the plan, no one was suppose to be hurt. It was only the dinosaurs that were supposed to get knocked around."

"Well, that's the way it goes sometimes," said Mitchell. "Look, sure you didn't mean for the guy to get hit on the head when you rigged that shelf so the model would fall, but that's the way it happened. And it's not so bad that Mr. Dinosaur was put out of commission for another half a day, either."

Fenton was shocked by what he had just heard. They were talking about his father! And it sounded as if the falling shelf *hadn't* been an accident, after all. Fenton peered quickly over the top of the boxes. There, standing only a few yards away, were the two men. And one of them was old Tom Williams from Galaxy!

Fenton gasped. Who would have thought that Tom Williams would turn out to be the spy? After all, he had been with Galaxy for years and years!

"Look," said the other man, the one who must be Nathan Mitchell, "do me a favor, old-timer, and go get me one of those cigars in my office."

"But you said I wouldn't have to do that kind of thing anymore if I came to work for Worldwide," said Tom. "You said I was going to get my own office and everything!"

"Yeah, yeah, I know what I said," said Mitchell. "Look, just go get me the cigar, all right?"

Tom's shoulders sank, and he shuffled off down the hall. Mr. Mitchell took out a toothpick and began to pick his teeth, gazing at the mechanical carnotaurus behind Fenton.

The man who had been pushing Dr. Beech around came into the room.

"Oh, hello, Mr. Mitchell," he said. "Listen, I got Doc tied up in one of those storage rooms back there, so just say when you want me to bring him out and make him work on this dinosaur."

"How's his attitude now, Bruce?" asked Mr. Mitchell, his toothpick still in his mouth. "A little more cooperative, I hope?"

"Oh, sure," Bruce answered with a grin. "I roughed him up a little, and he's ready to help us out all we want now."

Fenton shook his head in disgust. How could anyone beat up on a frail old man like Dr. Beech? These guys were the worst.

Just then Fenton thought he heard Justin's voice. Oh, no, he thought frantically. Don't come in here now, Justin. They'll catch you for sure.

But it was too late. Justin had already been caught. Fenton watched as he was dragged into the room by a man who could have been Bruce's twin.

"Well, well, what have we here, Brad?" said Mr. Mitchell.

"I found him in one of the offices," Brad answered. "He tried to hide under the desk, but I caught him."

"I can explain, I can explain," said Justin, trying to wriggle free of Bruce's grasp.

"Well, certainly then, go ahead and explain," drawled Mr. Mitchell. "I'd *love* to hear your explanation, sonny-boy."

"Well, I, uh, I—I got lost!" Justin blurted out.

"Lost?" Mr. Mitchell repeated.

He peered closely at Justin. "Something about you looks very familiar, kid."

Oh, no, thought Fenton. What if he recognizes Justin?

"He's lying, Mr. Mitchell," said Brad. "Let me teach him a lesson."

"Not yet," said Mr. Mitchell. "Let the boy finish. *Then* if I'm not satisfied you can teach him a lesson."

Fenton doubted very much that Justin was going to be able to come up with anything that could satisfy Mr. Mitchell. And Brad definitely didn't look like the kind of person you'd want to have teach you a lesson.

"Uh, I, um, well, you see, I was on a school trip," Justin sputtered.

Fenton looked around desperately. He had to think of a way to help Justin. And he had to do it right away, before Mr. Mitchell figured out who Justin was. Tom could come back with that cigar any minute and spill the beans. Fenton's eyes came to rest on the carnotaurus. It was a long shot, but it was all he could think of. He began to creep toward it.

"Yes, that's it," Justin went on. "I was on a trip with my class, and I got lost."

"On a trip to *my* studio?" said Mr. Mitchell doubtfully.

Fenton scurried toward the carnotaurus. Stepping up quickly onto a small stack of boxes, he lifted himself into the dinosaur's chest and slammed the hatch shut behind him.

"What was that?" demanded Mr. Mitchell.

"Nothing," said Justin quickly. "I mean, I don't know."

Fenton fumbled desperately with the dinosaur's controls. It really took two people to operate this thing. He'd only be able to make a couple of parts move at one time. But hopefully that would be enough.

He peered through the mesh-covered window and saw that both Brad and Bruce were holding on to Justin now.

"Ouch!" cried Justin. "Let go of me!"

"I smell something fishy about this kid," said Brad.

"Yes," said Mr. Mitchell, still chewing on his toothpick. "To be honest, so do I. Little boy, you look awfully familiar to me. And I don't give tours of my studio to school groups."

"Who are you, kid?" asked Bruce menacingly.

"Yeah," said Brad. "What are you doing here?"

Fenton reached for the nearest lever and pulled. There was a whirring sound, and he felt the dinosaur lurch forward.

"Hey!" said Bruce, his eyes growing wide. "Did you see that?"

Fenton reached for another lever. He could hear one of the dinosaur's arms moving just above him.

"It's moving!" cried Brad, stumbling backward.

"It's alive!" yelled Bruce, scrambling to get away.

"Don't be silly, you ninnies," said Mr. Mitchell. "Of course it's not—oh my goodness, it *is* moving! Quick! Get out of its way!"

As fast as he could, Fenton grabbed one lever after another, not even stopping to think. His only aim was to keep the carnotaurus in motion. Through the mesh-covered window he could see the three men shoving and pushing one another to get past the stacks of boxes and escape, and he thought he could hear Justin laughing somewhere nearby.

Then, off in the distance, he heard sirens. They were headed his way.

14

"It sure was nice of Ms. Cagney to give us this party," said Fenton, helping himself to another handful of potato chips.

"Well, son, she's very grateful to you for saving her movie the way you did," said Mr. Rumplemayer. "Although I must admit, I'm still not very happy about the fact that you told me you were going to do your homework with Justin when you weren't."

"I'm sorry about that, Dad," said Fenton. "But I had to do it. I mean, if I had told you the truth, that I wanted to go hide in the carnotaurus with Justin so we could catch the culprit, you would never have let me, and the movie never would have been saved."

"Well, I suppose you're right about that," said his father. "But I still don't want you to think it's all right to lie to me."

"I know it's wrong, Dad," said Fenton. It's just that once in a while I have to do it anyway, he added to himself.

"As long as we both understand," said Mr. Rumplemayer.

Fenton looked around the south wing, at the crowd that was gathered by the carnotaurus. There was Rosa Alvarez, sipping her drink and chatting with Harry Brown by the dinosaur's tail. Fenton almost couldn't believe that he had ever suspected them. Sitting nearby was Dr. Beech, who already looked much better than he had at Worldwide, and who had agreed to supervise the end of the film now that he was free. Nearby were Kim Alexander and Van Steele. Kim was wearing her sunglasses, and Van still looked a little nervous. On the other side of the room, talking to one of the computer animators, was Stolp. Fenton would miss Stolp and the others when he and his father went back to Morgan the next day. And he would miss being in Hollywood, too.

Fenton spotted Justin over by the food table. He waved, and Justin walked over.

"Well," said Fenton, grinning at his friend. "We did it."

"We sure did," said Justin. "Constance is really happy. She apologized to me about the ankylosaurid tail, and she said she wants to use me in her next movie, too."

"That's great," said Fenton.

"Yeah," said Justin. "It feels good to know I'm not automatically going to be blamed for everything that happens to go wrong around here. You know, it's funny, but I kept wondering why Tom never told Constance about that day he found us in her office."

"Yeah," said Fenton. "I guess it was because he wasn't supposed to be there then, either."

"Well, he won't be anywhere at Galaxy anymore, now that he lost his job," said Justin. "Constance says Tom must have been pretty unhappy here all these years to do something like that."

"I guess," said Fenton. "Although from what he said, it seemed like he used to like working for Galaxy. He just didn't like the way things are now."

"I know," said Justin. "Constance says he was nice to her back when she was a little girl. That he used to give her cinnamon sticks. I guess that's why she didn't want to see him go to jail."

"She definitely seemed pretty happy to have them lock Mr. Mitchell up, though," said Fenton.

"Are you kidding?" said Justin, snickering. "After the way you made that dinosaur move, I think even Mr. Mitchell himself was relieved when the police arrived."

"Yeah, I guess you're right," said Fenton, laughing.

"Hey, you know what I was thinking?" said Justin with a twinkle in his eye. "In a way what you did to those guys at Worldwide with the carnotaurus was the biggest practical joke of all time."

Fenton grinned. "Yeah, I guess it was," he agreed.

Ms. Cagney began to hit her fork against her glass.

"Attention, everyone!" she called.

The chatter in the room quieted down.

"On behalf of the cast and crew of *Night of the Carnotaurus*," Ms. Cagney began, "I want to thank to the Rumplemayers for all they've done to help us get this movie back on track."

There was a smattering of applause, and Fenton felt his cheeks get a little warm.

"Many thanks to Bill Rumplemayer, of course, for stepping in with his scientific expertise when we needed him," Ms. Cagney went on. "And a very, very special thank-you to Fenton, who has made sure that our movie will be a successful one after all. Now, Fenton, in order to show our appreciation, I have a little gift for you to take home with you. Could somebody bring it in, please?"

Two men carried in a dark blue canvas Galaxy chair. It was exactly like the ones Fenton had seen with the stars' names on them. Only this one said FENTON RUMPLEMAYER.

"Have a seat," said Ms. Cagney.

"Thanks," said Fenton, sitting down on the chair.

"Thank *you,* Fenton," she said.

Justin pulled a rolled-up paper from his pocket.

"Here," he said. "I have something for you too."

Fenton unrolled the paper. On it was a detailed drawing of himself and Justin sitting in the cockpit of the carnotaurus.

"It's my first dinosaur," said Justin.

"It's good," said Fenton. "You should draw more of them." Then he thought of something. "I have something for you, too." He reached into his jean jacket pocket and pulled out *The Pocket Book of One Thousand Interesting Dinosaur Facts.* "It's a really good book," he said, handing it to Justin.

"I guess it is," said Justin, grinning. "If you like dinosaurs."

Late the following afternoon, Fenton and his father exited the passenger area of the Cheyenne airport. Mr. Rumplemayer held the two suitcases, and Fenton carried his folded canvas chair in a slim cardboard box.

Fenton couldn't believe they had been gone only a week. So much had happened that, in some ways, Hollywood had almost started to seem like home to him. And now here he was, back in Wyoming. There was fresh snow on the ground, and their landing had been delayed half an hour while the runways were cleared. Even the airport felt colder than the one in Los Angeles.

Fenton heard a familiar voice from behind the barricade.

"Fen! Over here!"

He saw Maggie, along with Willy and Charlie. They were all waving wildly, and Owen, who was with them, was jumping up and down.

Fenton and his father made their way through the barricade and put their bags down on the floor.

"Hi, Fenton," said Willy excitedly. "How was it? Did you meet Van Steele?"

"Did you have a good time?" asked Maggie. "What's Hollywood like?"

"Here you go—I thought you might need these," said Charlie, handing over their winter jackets. "We're expecting a foot and a half more snow before Monday. Did you hear?"

As his father went to shake Charlie's hand, Fenton bent down to pet Owen.

"Boy," he said, looking up at Maggie and Willy, "do I have a lot to tell you guys."